"I don't need a bodyguard, since I'll be off the case," Janelle asserted.

"Wayne's men don't know that," Sawyer replied. "Nothing's changed."

"Except for everything," Janelle whispered.

"The only thing that's changed is your knowledge of the situation. The chief isn't going to suddenly treat you differently. Your brothers aren't."

Janelle looked at him with suspicion. "Why do you care?"

"I don't," he replied simply. "I just don't like illogical behaviour." And he liked the lost look in her eyes even less. "Now get up off the sofa and get out of those wet clothes."

He watched the smallest hint of a smile bloom on her lips. "Are you coming on to me, Detective?"

She'd caught him off guard with that. Maybe because ⬚⬚⬚⬚⬚⬚⬚⬚⬚⬚⬚⬚⬚⬚g of her i⬚⬚⬚⬚⬚⬚⬚⬚⬚⬚⬚⬚⬚⬚his assignm⬚⬚⬚⬚

"When ⬚⬚⬚⬚⬚⬚⬚⬚⬚⬚⬚⬚⬚ave to ask."

When. Not if, *when*.

Available in May 2007
from Mills & Boon Intrigue

Cavanaugh Watch

MARIE FERRARELLA

MILLS & BOON®

INTRIGUE™

MILLS & BOON and MILLS & BOON with the Rose Device are registered trademarks of the publisher.

First published in Great Britain 2007
Harlequin Mills & Boon Limited,
Eton House, 18-24 Paradise Road, Richmond, Surrey TW9 1SR

© Marie Rydzynski-Ferrarella 2006

ISBN: 978 0 263 85716 0

46-0507

Printed and bound in Spain
by Litografia Rosés S.A., Barcelona

MARIE FERRARELLA

This *USA TODAY* bestselling and RITA® Award-winning author has written over one hundred and fifty books, some under the name Marie Nicole. Her romances are beloved by fans worldwide.

Dearest Reader,

Here's the last of them – the last of the cousins – Brian's youngest, Janelle. I decided to do something a little different in this story, which is why I made Janelle…well, you'll find out. I don't know about you, but I'm going to be sad to see this lot go. During the last couple of years, the Cavanaughs provided a nice haven to turn to when the outside world got a little too crazy. And since I have tied up Andrew's story, I've been thinking that perhaps his younger brother, Brian, needed a lady to call his own, as well. Especially now that all his kids are grown and have found matches of their own. So I'm not altogether certain this is the last you've heard of the Cavanaughs after all. We'll see…

As always, I wish you much love in your lives.

Marie Ferrarella

To Bobbie Cimo and books that have
yet to be written.

Fondly, Marie

Chapter 1

To the untrained ear, it sounded very much like a car, backfiring. To the Cavanaugh ear, the noise sounded exactly like what it was.

A gunshot.

The shot was followed by several more rounds, fired in rapid succession.

Standing at the edge of the steps leading to the county courthouse, Janelle Cavanaugh automatically began turning in the direction of the sound, even as it was drowned out by screams and cries of distress and fear. She never completed the turn because, the next thing she knew, she was pushed to the ground so quickly the very air rushed out of her lungs.

Startled, she still had the presence of mind to protect

her head as she went down. This kept a concussion from becoming part of her medical history.

A man's body spread over the length of hers. A heavy body. Heavy, not in the sense that the person on top of her was fat, or even large boned. Just tall and muscular. And damn near overwhelming.

At first, she thought the man had been shot and was slumped over her. But then she felt his breath against the side of her face and along her neck. Whoever this lead weight was, he didn't breathe like a man struggling for air, or even one particularly taken aback by the preceding events.

"Stay down," the deep male voice ordered harshly when she tried to move. He made her think of a marine drill sergeant, one who took no prisoners, brooked no nonsense. She wondered if that was to mask his fear, or if he just liked bullying people.

Straining, Janelle listened. Growing up with three rambunctious brothers and seven cousins, most of whom were male, she had perfected the ability to hone in on sounds and isolate them. Amid the sounds of panic, she picked out the silence.

No more gunshots.

"Whoever was shooting's gone," she informed the man, who was covering her almost as closely as a lid fit over a pot. A man who, for all she knew, was just taking advantage of the situation, playing hero while he copped a feel. "So if you have the slightest notion of what's good for you, you'll get off me."

"A simple 'thank you' will do," the man growled in her ear.

The next moment, she felt his weight lessening. Her human shield rose to his feet and then offered her a hand. He did not offer her a smile.

Janelle felt a wave of antagonism rising up inside her. She ignored the hand, preferring to get up on her own power.

She was well-acquainted with the workings of a male mind and she could spot chauvinism. It was right there in the man's deep blue eyes. Janelle might have tossed her head a little as she got up. She was sorry she'd worn her blond hair up. The sight of a long mane flying over a shoulder always managed to underscore the look of disdain in her eyes.

Straightening her jacket, Janelle took in a deep breath. As the youngest of the chief of detectives' children and, at twenty-nine, the youngest assistant to the assistant district attorney in Aurora, Janelle was acutely aware that she was the target of a great deal of attention, not usually the welcomed sort.

She had, however, never been a target in the traditional sense of the word before.

You're not one, now, she told herself. *This probably has nothing to do with you.*

Still, she glanced down to make sure no holes existed in her anatomy that hadn't been there before she'd walked out through the courthouse's electronic doors. Her body felt numb—probably from having a lumpy torso land on it—but there was no searing pain. And other than smudges of dirt, she didn't have a mark on her.

When she looked up again, she saw that the man who'd thrown himself over her like a human blanket was doing the same. Checking her out. Slowly. She could almost feel his eyes pass coolly over her.

Janelle raised her chin. She was tempted to ask if he was looking for something. Or if he liked what he saw. But that would be opening herself up to a lot of things she didn't have time to deal with. The word *busy* in the dictionary came with her picture beneath it.

"Thank you," she said crisply, finally responding to his admonishment. She would have gotten around to thanking the lug for making like a superhero and she didn't appreciate being prompted.

Just the barest hint of a smile curved a mouth that seemed more accustomed to frowning. "Too bad today's not one of those scorchers. The ice might have come in handy, then."

Ignoring the man and his impossibly broad shoulders, Janelle began to take in her surroundings. There were eight people besides herself, the Human Shield and Assistant D.A. Woods on the courthouse steps. Eight people who had all scattered when the gunshots had come. All of them were out in the open, no better than clay ducks along a shooting gallery wall. Cover was a few steps down, at street level, or several steps back, inside the courthouse building.

She moved around the Shield, uncomfortably aware that the man was watching her.

And thinking what? Who the hell was he? She came across a great many people on the job. More at Uncle Andrew's house whenever the retired chief of police threw one of his many parties. To her recollection, she'd never seen this man before.

Because taking the initiative was what she'd been taught to do from a very early age, Janelle raised her voice and asked as calmly as possible, "Is anyone hurt?"

It took her a second to realize that Stephen Woods, the flamboyant assistant district attorney she had been working with since the beginning of the year, was just now getting to his feet.

She watched him uncertainly. The A.D.A. looked thoroughly shaken. "Stephen?"

Running his hand through hair that was just a little too black, Woods took a moment to pull himself together. He held up his hand, warding off her concern. "I'm all right, Janelle," he assured her. "And you?" he tagged on after a beat, as if he realized he'd been remiss.

She flashed a smile, brushing off a dried leaf from her straight navy blue skirt.

"Shaken, not stirred," she responded. Looking around, she saw that everyone began to get up. There were no sudden cries of anguish, no one screaming as if injured. In fact, the only upset had to do with frazzled nerves.

Thank God for small favors, she thought. "Looks like whoever was shooting had rotten aim."

"Or very good aim."

Janelle looked back at her shield. He was stripping

off the tie he'd had on. Stuffing it into his pocket, he offered another explanation for the hitless drive-by shooting. "Maybe 'whoever' just wanted to send a message to someone."

Since he'd left the statement dangling, Janelle pressed for an answer. "Which would be?"

There was no emotion in his eyes, she realized, and none on his chiseled features. No indication that he had just been through a harrowing experience, or even that it had left any sort of mark on him. The man obviously had ice water in his veins.

When he spoke, it could have been the voice of the shooter for all the inflection it held. "Toe the line, or next time, I won't miss."

Who the hell was he? Janelle wondered again. And was he tied to this somehow? "And that line would be?" she asked.

The broad shoulders beneath the tan sports jacket rose and fell carelessly. He wasn't quoting gospel, just the world as he knew it. "Don't testify, don't pursue the case, and don't dig too deep." His eyes met hers. "Take your pick."

It took her a second to draw her eyes away from his. She couldn't shake the feeling that she had just been scrutinized. Delved into. Janelle watched the stranger unbutton his collar. It made her think of a prisoner finally throwing open the door to his cell.

The image almost made her smile since it was a familiar one. Her brothers all hated wearing ties, which seemed rather ironic, given that they did it five days a week. More if the cases they were working necessitated their presence on days off.

Vehement dislike of anything formal was probably one of the main reasons her brother Jared had been so eager to volunteer to go undercover last year. He didn't have to be within spitting distance of a tie when he posed as a chef at a trendy restaurant suspected as a front for money laundering. His holiday from ties had gotten him a commendation when he'd nabbed the people responsible. It had also, indirectly, gotten him a wife.

That made Janelle the last of them. The last of the Cavanaughs who wasn't married or at least engaged to be married—if she didn't count her father. But Brian Cavanaugh had already been married once. For twenty-five years before his wife had died.

She herself had never gone that route. Had never pledged her heart to anyone, although she'd been mildly tempted once. With Barry, someone she'd met while clerking for Judge Teal, before she ever came to work for the D.A.'s office.

But whatever chances Barry might have had were aborted when he'd told her one night about wanting to "cut her out of the herd." The "herd" was the way he'd referred to her family. According to Barry, he felt as if he were competing against her family for her affections. An only child raised by parents who, as far as she could discern, made machines seem emotional, Barry couldn't fathom the concept of family loyalty. Moreover, he couldn't see why Sunday dinners—where everyone who could showed up at Uncle Andrew's spe-

cially made, oversize dining table to talk and catch up—
were so important to her.

Barry had become history before they could make
any. They had parted company almost two years ago,
when there were still a few single Cavanaughs left.

Now there was only her. And her dad, she thought
whimsically.

The next moment, Janelle mentally pulled back.
Where had that even come from? Maybe it was a theme
and variation of having your life flash before your eyes
when you were in a life-and-death moment. The only
problem with that theory was that she hadn't really been
aware of it being a life-and-death situation, until after
the last of the shots had died away.

Maybe this was a delayed reaction. It was as good
an explanation as any, she supposed. Not to mention, she
had trouble staying in the moment. Could be shock.

Her eyes were drawn back to the tall man in the tight
jeans and loose jacket who had thrown himself on top
of her. He had one of those faces that made you wonder.
Wonder where he'd been, who he was and what had left
its mark chiseled onto the planes and angles of his face.

She made a calculated observation. "You seem to
know a lot about these kinds of dire circumstances."

If she'd hit close to home, he never showed it. "Just
taking an educated guess."

Without a word of parting, he headed down the few
steps to the sidewalk and the parking lot beyond. As she
watched, wondering what to make of this man who had
been there for her in the right place at the right time, she

noticed him going toward a beaten-up vehicle. Its blue paint fading, the car had undoubtedly seen at least one complete rotation around the odometer, if not more.

Not someone high up on the crime food chain, Janelle decided.

"Are you all right, Nelle?"

The question came from behind her but she didn't have to turn around to see who the voice belonged to. Dax. When she did turn, she saw that her brother seemed genuinely concerned.

"I was just inside the building." He jerked his thumb at the electronic doors as he joined her.

Behind them at least a dozen people spilled out of the courthouse to see for themselves what was happening. The cry of "Shots fired!" had echoed over more than one walkie-talkie as bailiffs and security guards hurried into the center of the crowd.

She was vaguely aware that her brother was supposed to testify before a grand jury convened in one of the rooms on the second floor. These days, she was so busy, one of the few times she got to see her family was when their paths crossed during her workday.

She knew that Dax still tended to think of her as the little girl who had trouble tying the laces on her sneakers, instead of the quick-fisted tomboy who could sucker punch him at the drop of a hat. She silently prayed he wouldn't embarrass her in front of Stephen.

"I'm fine, Dax," she told him. "Really. Some guy threw himself on top of me at the first sound of shots. If anything, my bones are crushed, but the rest of me is intact."

Dax took hold of her shoulders anyway, as if he didn't trust her to tell him the truth. She did have a way of trying to brazen things out, which went back to the years when she had tagged along after him, Jared and Troy, determined not just to keep up with them but to show them up whenever possible. She knew she'd been the thorn in their sides, but they'd all been protective of her.

When she shrugged him off, he dropped his hands to his sides. "Good. Because I sure as hell didn't want to be the one to tell Dad that his baby girl got shot on the courthouse steps."

"How very touching," she quipped. "Thanks for the concern."

"Anytime." And then his expression grew serious as he looked over her head at the assistant district attorney. "Either one of you know of anyone who might have it in for you?"

"Other than my immediate family?" Janelle deadpanned. She followed it up with a "No," uttered a little too quickly. She realized her mistake the moment the word was out of her mouth. If she hadn't, the look on Dax's face would have alerted her. She knew that look. He didn't believe her.

At her side, Stephen shifted slightly.

Oh please, don't pick now to be straightforward with a question. Telling Dax anything about the major case they were handling would only make her older brother worry about her. And it wouldn't change anything. Certainly not her involvement in the case. The one that promised to be the biggest of her career so far. Perhaps the biggest one she would *ever* have. It was certainly big by any standards.

Anthony Wayne, the son of Marco Wayne, reputed first lieutenant within an organized crime network that had bedeviled all efforts to dismantle it for more than the last fifteen years, had been brought up on charges of possession of cocaine with intent to sell. The story went that the third-year premed student was supplementing his income with drugs, cutting into his father's turf, as it were.

As was usually the case, the D.A's office had come by their information purely by accident. Vice had busted a minor player who'd managed to land a decent public defender who'd finessed a deal for him. Sammy Martine, aka Sam Martinez, a two-bit criminal facing a third conviction and a lifetime of prison, had offered up Tony's name in exchange for a more lenient sentence that still had parole attached to it. The search warrant had turned up more than a kilo of cocaine in Tony's apartment. Vice had been waiting for Tony when he'd gotten home from classes and had arrested him. The case seemed airtight. A slam dunk that would put a feather in the hat of the D.A. and anyone else associated with the case.

Now that she'd had a couple of minutes to reflect, with the good Samaritan's deep voice echoing in her head, she knew that this could have been a warning from Tony's father to back off. To do whatever had to be done on their part to get the charges against Anthony dropped so that his son could once more be out on the street, a free man.

Not damn likely, Janelle silently vowed. It was going
to take more than a few bullets fired into the air to in-
timidate anyone at the D.A.'s office, even Stephen
Woods. For one thing, the district attorney was a
seasoned war veteran who had actually seen combat as
a young man. More than anything, he relished a good
fight. And this was a good fight. And as for Woods, he
saw it as his moment to shine.

Suddenly, Janelle could have sworn she saw a light
dawning in Dax's eyes.

Oh damn, he knew.

She should have known better than to hope that word
about the Wayne case wouldn't spread. It was almost a
given. Apparently there was no such thing as secrets in
the law-enforcement world. Somehow, things always
managed to leak out, at least to their own, despite the
best precautions. Wedded to the courts the way law enforcement was, there always seemed to be an overlap
of information. In the interest of keeping the informant
alive, the D.A.'s office had tried to keep the case under
wraps until it actually came to trial.

By the look on Dax's face, they'd failed. But she had
a feeling that her brother still might be in the dark about
who was going to be second chair on the case.

The position was hers.

She'd earned it. Not by coasting on her father's name,
the way some in the D.A.'s office—those who didn't
know her—maintained. But by working twice as hard
as anyone else in her position. It was the same kind of
situation her brothers all had faced. And her cousins, as

well. While she and her brothers were the children of the current chief of detectives, five of her cousins were the offspring of the former chief of police.

Only Patrick and Patience hadn't had to struggle out from beneath that sort of heavy mantle because their late father had never risen up through the ranks. Officer Michael Cavanaugh had been killed in the line of duty while still a uniformed patrolman. Even so, Patrick had still, on occasion, been accused of riding on his uncle's coattails. Only Patience had eluded that insult altogether. A veterinarian, Patience was the only one of them who had a "civilian" career. The only contact she had with the police department, other than at the table or with her husband, was when she cared for the force's K-9 squad.

Janelle had been given the position of second chair on the Wayne case a little more than two weeks ago as a reward for all the long hours and extensive work she'd put in since she had come to the D.A.'s office.

When Stephen Woods had called her into his office to tell her the news her first impulse had been to call home. To tell her father, her brothers, her cousins that she was finally getting somewhere.

Her second impulse had to do with family, as well. It had to do with shielding them because, even though they were all on the force, they tended to worry about one another. Because they all knew what could happen, knew all the ins and outs, all the chances that were taken and the odds of coming out unscathed.

It made surviving within the framework of the family difficult sometimes, especially as a female. But she knew she would rather struggle within that framework than live tranquilly outside of it. Being a Cavanaugh, living up to the family's standards, was of paramount importance to her. It always had been.

Dax frowned. "This is all about the Wayne case, isn't it?" It was a rhetorical question, posed to the A.D.A. rather than to her.

"Might be," Woods allowed.

"Or it might be an argument that got out of hand. Some guy getting even with someone who stole his girl," Janelle offered quickly, hoping to throw her brother off. "You won't know until you question everyone here." To make her point, she indicated the vehicle that her so-called protector was just about to enter. The dark blue sports car was old, but a classic. And small. From where she stood, getting into it didn't look as if it would be easy for him. Well over six feet tall, the man seemed almost as big as the car. "Including the guy who's just getting into that awful heap."

Chapter 2

Shifting slightly, Dax looked to where his sister pointed. He grinned and he shook his head.

"That's one person I wouldn't need to question in connection with this shooting if I were the investigating officer."

In the distance, the sound of sirens was heard. Obviously someone had already called 911.

There went lunch, Janelle thought, resigned.

She glanced at Dax, curious. What did he know that she didn't? It had always been that way between her and her siblings. Each always wanted to get a jump on the others, be the first to know, to do, to win. A sense of competition pulsated within all of them. And none so much as her.

"Why wouldn't you question him?" she asked.

Dax looked at the man finally getting into the vintage muscle car. "Because if he thought the shots were meant for him, he wouldn't be looking that complacent."

Janelle turned around and shaded her eyes, squinting as she peered into the parking lot and tried to make out his face. She'd seen more expression on the surface of a cut-glass vase.

She laughed shortly. "That's complacent?"

"Yeah."

She dropped her hand to her side and turned back to her brother. A squad car pulled up at the front of the courtyard and two uniformed officers emerged. Woods dropped back to speak to them.

And the questioning begins, she thought. Out loud she asked, "You know him?"

There'd been something about the man when she'd initially looked at him, an aura of danger mixed with an edginess close to the surface. She could readily believe that he was part of the same criminal network as Marco Wayne. But her brother didn't actually know anyone like that any more than she "knew" Tony Wayne. She had only met him once, at his arraignment. He'd looked like a scared kid and she'd almost felt sorry for him.

Dax nodded to one of the officers who looked his way as he answered his sister's question. "I know him. By sight and by reputation."

She tried not to let her impatience get the better of her. Dax didn't make it easy. "By reputation?" she echoed. "What is he, Zorro?"

He was doing this on purpose, she thought, dispensing information at the breakneck speed of an arthritic snail. When they'd been kids, this would have ended up with her bringing him down and sitting on him until he told her what she wanted to know. She doubted if Woods or the two officers would be very understanding if she tackled her brother on the steps of the county courthouse.

He laughed. "You hit closer than you think."

"Dax—" There was a warning note in her voice.

"That's Sawyer Boone." She looked at him blankly. The name meant nothing to her. "Detective Sawyer Boone," Dax elaborated. "He used to work under-cover—like Zorro." He laughed to himself. "First time I've ever seen him clean-shaven."

"Detective," Janelle repeated. "As in, the police force and not a P.I.?" Her brother nodded. "That would explain it."

"Explain what?"

She unconsciously rotated her shoulder. It felt a little sore. She had no doubt that by tomorrow, it would feel a lot sore. As probably would other parts of her anatomy. "When the shooting started, he threw himself on top of me."

Dax nodded, as if he'd expected nothing less. "He might have saved your life." They wouldn't know until the crime scene investigators determined where all the bullets had ultimately landed.

"He might have broken my neck," she countered. The man had been heavy. And quick. "Let's just call it a draw." She saw Dax shake his head at her. "What?" she asked.

"Someday you're going to have to admit that you can't single-handedly conquer everything."

Janelle patted his face several times with a hand that grew progressively heavier. "I'll let you know when that someday comes. You can bring the noisemakers and the party hats."

He laughed. "Count on it." As he spoke to her, Dax watched the officers take down information from the people who had been caught in the hail of bullets. "You're going to need protection."

The statement had come out of nowhere. Janelle refused to entertain the words seriously. "From Detective Boone?"

Dax wasn't smiling now. "From Wayne and his organization."

Oh no, don't you start worrying on me. It was bad enough she knew that their father was concerned about the element of people she dealt with. She didn't need this from her brother.

"We still haven't proven that he was even behind this," she insisted.

"Better to err on the side of caution—"

Caution was the last word she would have associated with Dax. When he was nine, he'd wanted to leap off the roof with a blue towel tied around his neck to see if he could fly. She'd been the one to run off to get their father before Dax could turn his dream into a reality.

"Since when?" she scoffed.

"Since I found out that the application form for getting a new sister was ten pages long," he cracked. He slipped his arm around her shoulders. "Besides, I don't want a new sister. I've spent too much time breaking you in. You're one of a kind, Nelle. They don't make them like you anymore. Thank God." Hooking his arm around her neck, he kissed the top of her head. "You need a bodyguard," he told her simply. "You and Woods as well as the witness he has stashed away."

So he knew about that, too. God, was nothing sacred? She supposed that most of the department had to know by now. And since, Internal Affairs would readily tell her, not every single member could be counted on to take the Boy Scout oath in complete sincerity, that meant that the so-called "secret" about bringing Tony Wayne to trial was an open one.

Had to happen sooner or later. She was just hoping for later.

Janelle pressed her lips together. As with everything else, she'd make the best of it. What other choice did she have?

But a bodyguard, well, that was another matter. She was not about to readily accept that as her fate. Not without a fight.

She glanced over toward the bottom of the concrete steps and saw that Woods was finished giving his statement to the officer. Her turn next, she supposed.

"If worst comes to worst, you and the family can all hold hands and rally around me," she quipped. "Until then, I have a case to prepare for." Which would happen right after she gave her statement, Janelle thought. She paused just long enough to tug on his sleeve in order to bring him down to her level. As he inclined his head, she kissed his cheek. "Goodbye, big brother. See you around."

"See you around," he echoed.

About to walk toward the officer closest to her, Janelle stopped in her tracks and turned back to look at Dax. She didn't like his tone. She'd been around him far too long not to be able to pick up on the nuances in her brother's voice. There was an underlying promise in it that she knew she wasn't going to be happy about. Did he plan on being her bodyguard? Or was he somehow going to be instrumental in finding a bodyguard for her?

Rather than call him on it, she let it go. Maybe if she ignored the threat, it would go away.

The next few minutes were spent telling the tall officer, Liam O'Hara, what she'd seen right before the shots. She had little to offer because she'd been engaged in conversation with the A.D.A. just before the gunman or gunmen had started shooting.

Officer O'Hara smiled politely as he made notations, then let her go. She almost flew down the steps to join Woods. She had a lot to do today before she could lock up her desk and drag her weary and progressively sorer body home tonight. If they were going to nail Tony Wayne for the crimes he was accused of, she had to make sure the nails were all straight and still available. Neither Woods nor their boss, D.A. Kleinmann, wanted any surprises at the trial once it got underway.

Ezra Kleinmann was the kind of man everyone noticed the moment he entered a room. There was nothing meek, nothing quiet about him. His mere presence spoke volumes even if he didn't utter a word. He had a bearing about him that proclaimed he was someone to be reckoned with. And never to be under-estimated or crossed.

For one thing, he stood six foot five. For another, he carried a formidable amount of weight on that frame. For the most part, this weight was evenly distributed, but no one was ever going to think of the once-famed criminal lawyer as being undernourished. When he spoke, it was with a booming voice and authority. And no one, if they wanted to advance within the offices of the district attorney, disregarded what he had to say. Ever.

But the moment she walked into his office and saw the look on Kleinmann's face, a part of Janelle began to rebel, expecting the worst. She knew something was coming. Something she wasn't going to like. Obviously someone—she was betting on Dax—had called the district attorney and informed him of the shooting incident before they had ever reached their destination. The moment she and Woods had returned to the building where the government offices were housed, they'd been immediately summoned to Kleinmann's office.

Sitting at the custom-made desk he'd brought with him when he'd first assumed office more than eighteen years ago, Kleinmann placed his wide palms on the edge of the blotter and leaned forward. His small, dark eyes managed to pin both of them at the same time. Daring them to speak anything but the truth.

"I heard there was a shooting."

"A drive-by," Janelle interjected, speaking up before Woods could confirm the D.A.'s statement and add his own dramatic embellishments.

Woods's eyes shifted toward her. "That's what they usually do when they drive by—unless they're tourists."

Kleinmann's thin lips just barely folded themselves into a smile. Playing the moment out, he steepled his fingers, then looked over them at the two people he had in his office. To the casual observer, he appeared calm. Janelle had learned by experience that nothing could be further from the truth. He was worried about them, she thought. God, she hoped he wasn't going to take her off the case. He was a Southern gentleman down to the bone and just politically incorrect enough to do it "for her own good."

After a moment, he made his ruling. "You two need bodyguards."

Woods nodded, looking relieved as he smiled. Janelle felt relieved, but for a different reason. At least this was better than being taken off the case. But she was far from happy about the turn of events. She hated nothing more than having her space invaded without an invitation.

She did her best to divorce the distress and annoyance she felt from her voice. "Is that really necessary, sir?"

Everyone knew that Kleinmann viewed himself as always being fair. They also knew he didn't like having his wishes questioned. "I believe it is."

The battle lines were drawn and she was on the other side. Janelle softly blew out a breath, knowing that she didn't have a snowball's chance in Haiti of winning this if it turned into any sort of debate.

"All right, I could probably get one of my brothers to…" But Kleinmann was shaking his large, sparsely haired head. His eyes were firmly fixed on her face, as if he were waiting for her to stop talking. Janelle backtracked. "What?"

The D.A. was well acquainted with her pedigree, knew most of her relatives by name and reputation. "You need someone around all the time," Kleinmann told her matter-of-factly. "Your brothers all have their jobs to do within their different departments. Besides, they're too close to you. You'd probably find a way to wrap them around your little finger." He forced a smile to his lips. On the whole, smiles did not arrive there naturally. "Don't worry, Ms. Cavanaugh, I've already got this covered."

Which was precisely why she *was* worried, Janelle thought. She did her best to keep her thoughts from her face. "So fast?"

"You don't get to be district attorney by sitting on your duff, waiting for your shoe polish to dry," he informed her tersely. His eyes shifted to include Woods as he continued. "And I don't want word getting around that the D.A.'s office can't take care of their own." His reasoning was simple. "If we let our own people become walking targets, how does that look if we tell a witness they have nothing to fear? That we'll protect them? Our credibility will go down the drain and we'll be out of business in no time. I have no desire to go back to private practice," he informed them glibly. His voice echoed about the spacious office, an office that was more than twice the size of any other on the floor. "I'm too old to start all over again."

As if he believed that, Janelle thought. She made the obligatory protest, knowing the D.A. expected it. "You're not too old, Ezra."

Kleinmann paused for a moment, as if enjoying the banter. "And you're not too subtle, Janelle." His eyes grew serious as he got back to business. "You're getting bodyguards, both of you," he underscored, looking at Janelle. "Along with Martinez or Matine, or whatever he wants to call himself. I've already put the requisition in."

Going through channels would take time. Janelle felt a ray of hope. "The wheels of justice grind slowly."

With any luck, she thought, by the time the bodyguards were assigned, the D.A. would change his mind about their necessity. She absolutely hated the idea of having a shadow dogging her every movement. Pointing things out to her that even a hopeless simpleton would know.

She found herself wishing that one of her brothers *could* be given the assignment. But now that she thought of it, neither Dax nor Troy nor Jared handled that kind of thing. Her father would have to be brought into this in order to make the arrangements.

God, that was the *last* thing she wanted, to bring her father into this. He'd want to wrap her in a six-foot cocoon.

Like a man engaged in a mental game of chess, one that

he was winning, Kleinmann permitted himself a fleeting smug look. "Not this time." The smug look widened to resemble a smile. "Not when you know who to call."

And she had no doubt that the D.A. knew exactly who to call. And how to get someone to do what he wanted when he wanted it. A great many people in Aurora owed him favors. She knew damn well that any kind of protest voiced on her part was useless and might even work against her. You didn't go far in this office if you got on D.A. Ezra Kleinmann's bad side. And you got there one of two ways. By consistently losing cases or by going up against him.

She knew enough to pick her battles carefully. Her father had taught her that. It was one of the first lessons she'd ever learned.

Brian Cavanaugh had taught her something equally important, as well: how to lose graciously. Not that losing had ever been a large factor in Brian Cavanaugh's professional life. Personally, however, was another story. He'd lost his wife of twenty-five years, a woman he had looked forward to spending the rest of his natural life with. The loss had been difficult to come to terms with. It caused him to teach his children to be prepared for the worst—just in case.

This was one of those times to step back from the line of scrimmage. Janelle forced a smile she in no way felt. Protesting being assigned a bodyguard, someone who would perforce intrude into the fabric of her life, imposing his will over hers, might be useless, but no one said she had to like it.

"How soon are we getting the bodyguards?" Woods asked.

He sounded eager and relieved, Janelle thought. Relieved that he didn't have to appear as if he were less than manly because he really wanted someone watching his back until this case was over.

She knew that had been on the assistant D.A.'s mind for the last half hour. It had been apparent in their conversation as they'd returned from the courthouse. She'd asked him several questions regarding the finer points of some of the procedures they were implementing. The answers she'd gotten had been rendered by a man whose thoughts were severely distracted and scattered.

Growing up with three brothers had made her competitive. It had also made her motherly on occasion. She felt the A.D.A's discomfort, both over the threat and at his reaction to it.

Changing direction, she'd abruptly asked, "Wasn't that Adam Shepherd I saw outside the courthouse just before the gunshots went off?"

Her question had sliced through the fog and Woods had looked at her. "Yes."

She grinned. Shepherd was a highly sought after divorce lawyer famed for getting his clients exorbitant alimony settlements.

"So maybe the shooter was a disgruntled ex-husband looking to get revenge because Shepherd had raked him over the coals."

Woods had looked at her then, a tired smile on his

lips, as if to tell her that he knew what she was up to. "I don't think so, Janelle. But it's a nice theory."

"Might be more than a theory. People surprise you sometimes."

He'd nodded, looking directly at her. "Yes, they do."

Now, without waiting for further comment or questions, the D.A. pressed a button on his telephone console. "Doris, send the two gentlemen in."

A soft, disembodied voice informed him, "There's only one here, sir. A Detective Novak."

Kleinmann frowned. "Where's the other?"

"Hasn't gotten here yet, sir," Doris told him. "But he did call in," she added, "said he'd be here shortly. Had something to do first."

The frown on Kleinmann's brow deepened as he released the button.

Not that the D.A. said anything outright, but Janelle could see that the vein in his neck was a bit more prominent than usual. That was always an indication for those who worked with the D.A. to tread lightly until the vein returned to its normal size.

The door to the D.A.'s inner office opened and an average-looking man with dark brown hair and a nondescript, slightly wrinkled suit entered.

Detective Novak, Janelle thought.

The man looked vaguely familiar. Their paths had crossed somewhere along the line, she assumed. When their eyes met, she nodded at him.

The detective went on to extend his hand to the D.A. "John Novak, sir."

Kleinmann took the hand that was offered. "Detective Novak, this is Assistant District Attorney Stephen Woods. It'll be your job to see that not a single one of the many hairs on his head come to any harm. That goes for the rest of his body, as well." The D.A. permitted himself a very dry chuckle.

The chuckle was blotted out by the sound of a door being opened and then closed in the outer office. A quick exchange of voices followed. The look on Novak's face indicated that he recognized the voice of the person who had entered.

Her bodyguard, probably.

Bracing herself, Janelle turned around. Only to discover that she wasn't quite braced enough. Walking into the D.A.'s office was the very same man who had thrown himself on top of her less than an hour ago.

This day, she thought grimly, just kept getting worse and worse.

Chapter 3

Sawyer made no attempt to mask his displeasure, no attempt to allow his facial muscles to relax out of their current frown.

Other than undercover work when it was necessary, sometimes even to save his own life, Sawyer didn't believe in lying. The way he saw it, looking pleased right now would have been lying.

He didn't much like the idea of being asked to babysit. Which was how he saw his new assignment. He was too old for that and too experienced to be wasted on a menial detail. And to Detective Sawyer Boone, a not-so-recent LAPD transplant, that was exactly what being a so-called bodyguard for some bit of fluff currently attached to the district attorney's office was: the job of glorified babysitter.

Sawyer wasn't looking to be, nor did he want to be, a glorified anything. He wanted to be on the streets, working undercover. Facing life-and-death situations where maybe, just maybe, death would someday be the viable alternative.

That way, he wouldn't have to do it himself. Wouldn't have to actually take his own life. There didn't seem to be another way to end the unending onslaught of nightmares. The nightmares that haunted him both waking and sleeping. Nightmares about Allison.

Allison had been senselessly wiped out less than a month before their wedding, killed because she'd been in the wrong place at the wrong time. While two worthless pieces of scum had been trying to even some imaginary score.

She'd been in her car, stopped at a light, when she'd been caught by a stray bullet during a drive-by shooting. A gang member had peppered a rival gang member's home. And snuffed out his Allison's life.

If Allison hadn't been so damn altruistic, if she hadn't been part of that free legal aid firm, if she'd just gone into practice with that Beverly Hills firm that had wanted her instead of following in her father's footsteps, she would be here today.

Or rather, Sawyer thought, his expression dark as he looked from one person to the other in the D.A.'s office, he would have been there. With her. Living with Allison in Southern California instead of here, being asked to do stand guard over the chief of detectives' little darling because the woman had been spooked by the sound of gunfire.

His superior, Lieutenant Richard Reynolds, had been waiting for him when he'd gotten back from testifying in court. At first, he'd thought the man had been just making conversation, informing him of what he'd just heard had happened. Maybe even waiting for Sawyer to fill in the details. But it had very quickly become apparent that he was being given an assignment. The only kind of assignment he would have turned down. If he'd been given a choice, which he hadn't.

The incident had taken place less than an hour ago and already the call for bodyguards had been put out and filled. No paperwork or red tape to impede anything.

Apparently, he thought cynically as his eyes washed over the petite blonde in the navy suit, when necessary, things moved fast within the halls of the Aurora police department.

Protesting the assignment would do no good. He'd just wrapped up a case and was considered free. The fact that he didn't have a relationship of any sort with the woman or any of her family was considered a plus.

"She's a mite headstrong, I hear," Reynolds had told him. "All the Cavanaugh women are," he'd added after lowering his voice. "The D.A. requested someone she couldn't bully into her way of thinking."

Well, that was him, all right. He wasn't about to be bullied by anyone, least of all a woman who thought her name earned her privileges.

Sawyer took slow, careful measure of her now, the

way he would have any assignment he'd been given, any person he encountered on the job. Survival usually depended on observation.

He had to admit that, at about five-four, with no spare meat on her bones and honey-blond hair worn up and away from her face, the woman was fairly easy on the eyes. But it wasn't his eyes that concerned him. He had no desire to be a glorified babysitter under any circumstances and, while the crime organization in question was a formidable one, he was of the personal opinion that what had happened in front of the courthouse an hour ago was an isolated incident, meant as a warning, nothing more.

The man Marco Wayne bore allegiance to was not about to waste money or manpower getting into an unofficial war with the members of the Aurora police department or the district attorney's office over some lowlife, even if that lowlife *was* Marco's son. Marco Wayne had to be acting on his own. And treading a very fine line. In order not to do anything that would put him in disfavor with his boss, or jeopardize his own life, he would have only done something to shake up the D.A.'s office, nothing more.

And the sooner he was done with this assignment, the better, Sawyer thought.

Janelle's eyes met the detective's. The connection was instantaneous. She could read his every thought. And it wasn't flattering.

Janelle squared her shoulders.

Damn but this man thought he could walk on water. It was evident in his eyes, in his expression, in his very gait as he strode into the office. If anything, the man looked even more surly now than he had when he'd pushed her down onto the pavement.

And covered her body with his own, she reminded herself.

Even at her most annoyed, she always tried to be fair. And the truth was, she supposed, she owed this man. She could have been seriously hurt, or worse, if he hadn't shielded her.

Only in the recesses of her mind did she admit to herself that she wasn't the superwoman she pretended to be. Janelle frowned. Being somewhat in debt to him, however unintentionally and however unwillingly, meant that she couldn't protest too loudly about his being assigned to be her bodyguard.

Damn, she thought again.

She shifted her eyes over toward the man whose name appeared on her paychecks.

"Do you *really* think this is necessary?" she asked, trying to appeal to his legendary frugal nature. This kind of thing cost the department more than just a little money. "Maybe we're overreacting." She said *we* and hoped that it wasn't overly evident that she actually meant that *he* was overreacting.

Kleinmann beckoned her over to his desk. Feeling a little foolish, bracing herself for a lecture, she came forward. Her boss lowered his voice, as if to keep it from carrying to the other three occupants of the room. Of them, she noticed that only Woods seemed to be straining a little to hear what was coming next.

Her detective looked like a stone statue. He wasn't even blinking. Dutifully, Janelle leaned in toward the D.A.

"Your father would cut off my head and have it mounted on a pike in the middle of the city if I ignored this incident and then something wound up happening to you."

"If anything did—which it won't," she interjected, "I'd take the blame, tell him it was my fault. That I refused protection."

The look on Kleinmann's face told her she might as well have been reciting *The Iliad* in the original Greek for all the impression she was making on him with her rhetoric. Kleinmann had made up his mind and there was no budging him.

Having her father as important as he was in the hierarchy of the police department was at times more of a curse than a blessing. She was proud of him, but there was no denying that she'd put up with her share of grief because of who he was, as well. Her own pride and determination had never allowed her to take advantage of the Cavanaugh name, but that never stopped people from thinking she'd advanced quickly because she was the daughter of the chief of detectives and had prevailed on her father to fast-track her.

It was damn frustrating. She expressly didn't mention anything that went on in the D.A.'s office whenever she did get together with her father.

There were times like this, when she was made to pay the price of nepotism without ever having reaped any of the rewards, that almost made her wish she *had* taken advantage of the Cavanaugh name. She knew that the thinking was, with so many of her relatives embedded in law enforcement, and her cousin Callie even married to a judge, there wasn't anything she couldn't get done, no ticket not taken care of.

Except that she didn't work that way, hadn't been raised that way. None of them had.

Virtue is its own reward, her father had taught her. It had to be, she thought now, because nothing else sure as hell was.

Janelle struggled to suppress a resigned, less-than-thrilled sigh. Didn't matter if she was raised that way or not, she was going to wind up being made to pay for just having the Cavanaugh name.

Okay, she could make the best of this, Janelle told herself. Or at least be civil.

Turning toward the man fate and the D.A. seemed determined to saddle her with, she put her hand out to him. "So, I guess you and I are going to be spending some time together."

He looked down at her hand and after a beat shook it once before dropping it. The man acted as if any contact outside of the line of duty was distasteful to him. "I guess so."

Oh, this is just going to be a barrel of laughs, Janelle thought.

And how was it possible, unless you were some sort of a trained ventriloquist, to utter words without moving your lips? she wondered, dropping her hand to her side. Her unwanted bodyguard seemed to be communicating through clenched teeth and barely moving his lips. If she didn't know better, she would have said that he was using mental telepathy. Except that it was obvious to her that she wasn't the only one who had heard the deep, rumbling voice.

She found it difficult to keep her annoyance under wraps, but she was determined not to make any undue waves. When she'd signed on to the D.A.'s office, she'd known it wouldn't be all fun and games, that there would be times she'd find trying, but she'd just assumed it would have to do with the workload and hours spent, not with having to put up with Darth Vader's better-looking cousin.

Her eyes shifted toward Kleinmann. The man looked rather satisfied with himself for some reason. Sure, why not? He wasn't the one who had to put up with this tall, hulking shadow.

"How long?" she asked.

"Until the trial is over." Kleinmann appeared to consider his answer, then added, "Maybe longer."

Janelle's eyes widened. Was this some kind of torture devised for assistants to the A.D.A.? Like an initiation for a fraternity?

She glanced over toward the assistant district attorney, hoping to get an inkling of support. But Woods didn't seem put off by the idea of having a constant companion wherever he went. Well, maybe he didn't mind, but she did. A line had to be drawn somewhere, didn't it?

"Longer?" she echoed, staring at Kleinmann. "Why longer?"

"Retaliation—for when we do convict," he added in a voice that refused to entertain the possibility of anything less than a conviction. No one liked to lose, but Kleinmann had made it known that he passionately hated it.

"Maybe I can get his lawyer to accept a plea," Woods suggested.

Kleinmann shook his head. "I doubt it. Not after he hears about the attempted shooting. He'll feel as if his side has all the marbles."

"It's not about marbles," Janelle interjected. "It's about justice." She saw Sawyer roll his eyes. Was that contempt she saw on his face, or just badly displayed amusement? She turned on him, her patience at an end. "What? You have something to say? Why don't you say it out loud, Detective Boone, so that the rest of us can share in your wisdom?"

He'd never liked being singled out, not when he'd worked in L.A. and not here. He was one of those people who wanted no attention, craved no spotlight. He just wanted to do his job and go home.

"Nothing," he bit off.

She had to be satisfied with that. Until after the D.A. had dismissed them from his office. Once outside Kleinmann's door and clear of his secretary, a woman who had the hearing range of a bat, Janelle abruptly stopped walking and turned to the man at her side.

"Why did you roll your eyes back there?"

She'd thrown him off by stopping and by the antagonistic tone in her voice. He had no desire to engage her in conversation or to have any exchange of ideas. This woman was his assignment, just like infiltrating a local drug dealer's gang, following the trail to the top, had been his assignment, the one that had brought him to court this morning.

Except that with the latter, he'd assumed a persona, had come up with a speech pattern, a background for himself, a made-up life he'd stepped into. Here, he was supposed to be Sawyer Boone, a detective on the APD, and he didn't do all that well as himself. Because being himself meant sharing, something he'd only done successfully once in his life, and she was gone.

"You don't want to know," he told her.

Now there was a chauvinistic answer if ever she'd come across one. Raised with and around as many males as she had been, Janelle still had never experienced chauvinism in its truest sense. She was tested as a person, as a Cavanaugh, not as a female in a male world.

"If I hadn't wanted to hear the answer, Detective Boone," she told him evenly, "I wouldn't have asked the question."

He watched her for a long moment, as if he was weighing something. And then he said, "Because if you think any of this is about justice, you're more naive than you look."

Her eyes narrowed as she asked, "And just how naive do I look?"

Sawyer snorted. "Like you could be their poster girl."

Normally, being referred to as a *girl* didn't rankle her. She had no problem with the word because she had no problem with her self-esteem. And anyone who knew her knew what kind of mettle she was made of. But for some unknown reason, everything out of this man's mouth, including probably *hello,* promised to rankle her. Clear down to her bones.

She didn't waste her breath denying his statement or reading him the riot act because of it. She had a bigger question on her mind. "If you find this assignment beneath you, why didn't you protest when you were given it?"

"I did," he answered simply. Sawyer led the way to her office on the other end of the building. He obviously already knew the layout of their floor, she thought. "I got overridden."

"That makes two of us," she told him. Sawyer looked at her and she could have sworn she detected a hint of surprise in his eyes. "I guess then," she continued, "this is something we both will just have to suffer through."

Sawyer said nothing. He barely nodded in response to her last statement, hiding his surprise that someone he'd just naturally assumed had been spoiled within an inch of her life would balk at being offered protection from the "bad guys."

Unless something wasn't kosher here. Maybe this was a publicity stunt on her part to attract attention to the case. Maybe she was after a change of venue and this sort of thing could just do it. Not unheard of.

"For the record," she said as they reached her office door, "I don't want you here as much as you don't want to be here."

For the first time since he'd rescued her, the corners

of his mouth curved up just a fraction. "I really doubt that, Cavanaugh."

Without making a comment, Janelle opened the door and walked into the office she affectionately called her *cubbyhole*. It was no more crammed and cluttered now than it had been before she'd left for the courthouse this morning. But somehow having an extra body with her cut down on her space. She hadn't minded when Woods had given the tiny office to her. She didn't require much.

But there was hardly any room within the enclosure to stuff in another book, much less a warm body that was larger than hers by a long shot.

She glanced around, trying to see the area through his eyes. "I really don't know where you're going to hang around," she finally said.

"Don't worry about it, I'll take care of me. And you," he added after a slight pause.

She felt as if she were being put on notice. And she didn't like it. Didn't like not feeling in charge. Control was a very, very important thing to her, something she had had to fight for ever since she could remember. That, and respect. It had been awarded within her household, but not automatically. You received respect when you earned it. This new speed bump in her life was going to be one hell of a challenge to surmount.

She indicated a chair that was against the wall. "I guess you can sit there."

Sawyer grabbed the top of the chair, swinging it over to the side of the desk without saying a word. He planted the chair, not himself.

Just then, the phone rang and she almost sighed with relief. Something to draw her attention away from how very crammed and how very close the lack of space within the room made everything feel.

Hand on the receiver, she cleared her throat before raising it to her ear. Her voice was crisp when she spoke. "Cavanaugh."

There was silence on the other end. For a minute, she thought whoever was calling had dialed a wrong number. But there was no hurried hang-up, no muttered apology, no uncertain voice asking to speak to someone she'd never heard of.

She tried again. "Hello?"

This time, someone did speak. "Is this Janelle Cavanaugh?"

The deep resonant voice vibrated against her ear. She listened closely, wondering if this was one of her brothers or male cousins, playing a trick on her. "Yes, this is Janelle Cavanaugh."

There was another pause, as if whoever it was on the other end of the line was absorbing her voice. "He's innocent."

She frowned, definitely not in the mood to play along. "Who is this?" she demanded. Out of the corner of her eye, she saw Sawyer become alert.

"This is Marco Wayne," the man on the other end informed her. His voice was strong, but laced with emotion. That surprised her. "My son is innocent."

"Mr. Wayne—" The moment she said her caller's name, Sawyer drew closer to her. The look on his face was hard, as if he expected a bomb to be transmitted across the telephone wires. Annoyed by the lack of privacy, she turned her body away from him, only to have him circle in front of her.

Great, she thought, there was no getting away from him. This was *not* going to work.

"Mr. Wayne," she repeated, "this is highly inappropriate. You can't be calling me about this. About anything," she added quickly before he could protest.

If she meant to cut him off, she failed. "I'm calling because you're involved in this trial and I want you to understand that my son had nothing to do with what he is accused of."

"If he didn't do it," she said for form's sake, because everything they had pointed to Tony's guilt, "he'll be proven innocent."

"Not with the evidence that was planted against him," Wayne countered. "He was framed."

She wasn't about to stand here, arguing with the man. "I'm hanging up now, Mr. Wayne."

There was an urgency resonating in the voice against her ear. "I just want what every father wants for his son—a fair chance."

Janelle pressed her lips together. She knew damn well that she should be disconnecting the call. Every rule demanded it. This was highly unprofessional and unethical. But although she willed it, her hand did not replace the receiver in the cradle, did not disconnect the call. She couldn't seem to help herself.

The man sounded sincere.

She supposed that was why he'd gotten as far as he had, being able to get to people, to bend them to his will. One way or another.

She tried once more. "And you'll get it. The D.A.'s office has no intentions of railroading anyone, Mr. Wayne. You son is going to be given a fair trial. You have my word on it."

The man on the other end was not finished. "Talk to that scum of a witness again. He's lying. If you offer him a deal, he'll say anything you want him to." There was a pause. "Tell him that Marco Wayne will make sure he burns in hell if his son is harmed."

Anger flashed in her eyes. "I'm not a conduit for your threats, Mr. Wayne."

It was the last thing she said to the man before Sawyer disconnected her.

Chapter 4

For a second, everything seemed to freeze around her. Janelle didn't believe what had just happened, what she was seeing. Sawyer with his finger pressed on the black telephone cradle, pushing the button down flat. Disconnecting her from the man she'd been speaking to.

Who the hell did this jerk think he was?

It didn't matter that she was about to terminate the call herself, that she hadn't wanted to talk to Wayne in the first place. All that mattered was that this so-called bodyguard she neither wanted nor felt she needed had decided to take it upon himself to exercise his will over hers.

He had a lot to learn about dealing with a Cavanaugh.

It was all Janelle could do to keep from throwing the receiver she was holding at his head. Instead, she threw it down hard into the cradle. The impact caused it to bounce back out. She glared as Sawyer replaced it. He was acting as if nothing out of the ordinary had just transpired.

She swung around to face him. There were less than two inches of viable space between them. "What the hell do you think you're doing?"

Maybe it was his imagination, but he could almost feel the heat sizzling between them. This was one angry woman. Not to mention reckless.

"Saving you from improper conduct charges," Sawyer replied mildly. He paused, as if thinking the matter over. "Maybe even saving your butt."

Her eyes narrowed. "I can take care of my own butt, thank you," she informed him icily. "The only thing your job calls for is blending in with the scenery and, on the off chance that some time during our hopefully short association there might be a bullet hurtling toward me, throwing yourself in front of me so that the bullet gets you and not me. However, until that bullet does come hurtling toward me, I would be grateful if you just find a way to fade into the shadows—and keep your hands at your sides."

Stripping off his sports jacket, he hung it over the back of his newly acquired chair. The muscles on his chest and arms seemed to have a life of their own as they rippled and flexed. Janelle tried not to notice, but they were even more impressive than the holster and weapon he wore strapped to his upper torso.

"You through?" he asked, his eyes never leaving her face.

Janelle lifted her chin, a fighter not about to give an inch. "For now."

"Talking to Wayne like that is enough to get you thrown off the case and most likely out of the D.A.'s office if anyone finds out—unless 'Daddy' can pull some mighty strong strings for you."

The smug bastard. Right about now, she found herself wishing that her father was able to pull a noose, not a string. Tightly.

Janelle blew out a breath, refusing to lose it and let this cocky detective think he got to her.

"For the record," she told him evenly, her voice flat in order to retain control over it, "'Daddy' has got nothing to do with my career, how far I advance or *don't* advance. We happen to share the same last name and the same genes. He did not get me here and he cannot keep me here if Kleinmann is unhappy with my work." She raised her head and unconsciously rolled forward on her toes because, even in her four-inch heels, she was at least a half foot shorter than Sawyer was and it galled her. "Do I make myself clear?"

He let his eyes wash over her slowly, thoroughly, before saying, "Yes."

The man was mocking her, Janelle thought, but she couldn't very well say that without sounding as if she were just this side of crazy. A Neanderthal like Boone would probably say something about it being her time of the month rather than the fact that he was an insufferable jerk.

"Oh, and one more thing," she added, her tone deceptively calm.

About to sit down, Sawyer looked her way and raised an eyebrow. "Yes?"

She did her best not to raise her voice. There was a knock on the door, but she ignored it until she finished making her point. "Don't you ever, *ever* do something like that again."

"And if I do?"

"I'll cut off your hand."

Tough, he thought, appraising the petite woman before him. He wondered if that was because of her last name or because it was inherent in her nature. "I'll keep that in mind."

Janelle could literally feel her back going up. Damn, what had she done to have this jackass thrust into her life?

"Do that." Whoever was on the other side of her door knocked again, just as timidly as the first time. "What?" Janelle shouted before she could catch herself.

The next moment, the door opened slowly, as if the person on the other side wasn't sure if it was safe to come in.

Mariel Collins stuck her head in. Appointed to the A.D.A. six months ago, the tall, dark-haired young woman walked into the room as if she were literally treading on eggshells, afraid of damaging even one of them.

Her brown eyes looked down at the papers she was holding before she extended them to Janelle.

"Um, this just came in for you. I thought you might

want to see it." There was no conviction in her voice, just an appeal for understanding.

In her hand, Mariel held one of the dreaded blue-bound notices. Once unfolded, they were always found to contain motions to suppress inside of them. Everyone at the D.A.'s office hated the sight of them because they always moved to suppress evidence crucial to making a case.

Blue, once her favorite color, was swiftly becoming her least favorite, Janelle thought. With a sigh, she crossed to Mariel, who had still not gone any farther than the threshold, and took the folded papers from her.

Opening them, Janelle scanned the papers quickly. "Damn."

"Bad news?" Mariel asked nervously. Her mouth twitched in a sickly smile as her attempt at conversation fell flat.

Janelle squelched the urge to crush the papers in her hand. Instead, she tossed them on top of her desk. "Wayne's lawyer is moving to suppress his client's BlackBerry."

Mariel looked at her, perplexed. "Suppress his cell phone?"

"No, his handheld PC," Janelle corrected. Damn it, she should have known things were going too well. The BlackBerry contained a detailed journal that confirmed their informant's information. "That had all the names of Tony's customers on it. It helped tie him up with a big red bow." She frowned as she perused the legal document again. The words refused to change. "He's calling it inadmissible evidence."

"How did you obtain it?"

The question came from Sawyer. She looked at him over her shoulder. She knew what he was thinking.

"Not by tossing the apartment." That was probably the way he operated, but not the detectives who had brought Wayne in. "The arresting detective said it was cold outside and that when he made the arrest, Wayne asked for his jacket. It was on a chair next to his desk. When the detective got it for him, the BlackBerry fell out of one of the pockets."

"And right at his feet." Sawyer smirked. "Convenient."

She felt a surge of anger. "Are you accusing the arresting detective of something?"

Her eyes flashed when she was angry, he noted. And they turned from a medium green to a darker shade that was almost emerald. Didn't take much to get her going. "Why?" he asked mildly. "Are you related to the arresting detective?"

She didn't like what he was implying. And she didn't much like him. "No. But I happen to believe in the integrity of the Aurora police department."

Being part of a team had never interested him. If you relied on people, they generally let you down. Usually when you needed them most. Like his parents had, divorcing and deserting him before his seventh birthday. "I'd guess you'd have to, wouldn't you?"

She had had just about enough of this man's veiled comments and cryptic words. "What's that supposed to mean?"

Instead of answering right away, Sawyer swung the

chair with his jacket on it around so that the back faced her. He straddled it. "Judging from the evidence, you're bright enough to put two and two together. I don't think I have to explain it to you."

Janelle realized that by now, Mariel had faded back across the threshold and was in the corridor. The next moment, the woman closed the door, sealing them in together.

They were alone. And that made her temper harder to hang on to. She did her best, clenching her hands at her sides so hard, she wound up digging her nails into her palms in an effort to sound calm.

"Try." It wasn't a request; it was an order.

After a beat, with a slight incline of his head, he obliged her. "With so many members of your family on the force, if there was dirt, it might rub off on one of them." He made it sound elementary. "So you pretend there isn't any."

Janelle opened her mouth to retort, then shut it without saying a word. He was putting her on the defensive. One of the first lessons her father had ever taught her was to keep her opponent from backing her into a corner. The best way to do that was to go on the offensive. Growing up with her brothers and cousins had given her a great deal of practice.

She took a long, deep breath, then exhaled before asking, "How long have you had this dark view of the world, Detective Boone?"

If she meant to rattle him, she didn't succeed. "Ever since I could remember."

It was a lie, because he vaguely remembered a time when there had been hope. When the world had not come in dark colors. But then his parents had gone their separate ways and he'd been shipped off to his mother's mother, a woman who was far more interested in strange men than in raising him. Except for the small space of time when Allison had been in his life, he'd been alone for a very long time.

Janelle studied him. He meant it, she realized. The thought almost made her shiver. The man had to be hollow inside. She would have felt sorry for him—if he didn't make her so angry. "And you anticipate the worst."

There was just the slightest nod of his head. "That way I'm never disappointed. And I'm not."

What an awful way to face life. She wasn't like her cousin Patience, who had this overwhelming desire to fix every hurt animal that limped across her line of vision. But she hated seeing a tortured soul and that was what she was looking at, Janelle thought. A soul that had been through torture. He'd said something about being this way ever since he could remember. There was only one reason for that.

"What kind of a childhood did you have, Detective Boone?" she asked him.

His eyes met hers. He bit off the inclination to tell her to mind her own business. Instead, he said, "I didn't."

She nodded, as pieces moved into place. "That would explain it."

Janelle was surprised to see his mouth curve ever so slightly into a smile. But by no means was it a warm smile, nor did it involve any part of him other than the skin on his lips. His eyes didn't smile. They remained detached, cold. Analytical.

Robots had eyes like that, she thought. In high-tech science-fiction movies. Intelligent, but without a soul, without compassion—because they had no frame of reference available against which to measure feelings. Was that the case with him?

The cold smile faded as if it had never existed. "Don't try to analyze me, Cavanaugh. Your talents would be best used elsewhere."

There was another knock on the door. A firm one this time. Before she extended an invitation to come in, the door was opened, bringing with it a smattering more air, not exactly fresh, but every little bit helped right now, she thought.

Janelle drew in a lungful, as if that would somehow help her deal with Sawyer and his all-encompassing disdain. She looked at the sensibly dressed young woman in the doorway. "Yes?"

Another one of the assistants. Marcia Croft had been there three weeks longer than Janelle had and was still trying to direct Stephen Woods's attention over in her direction. It was no secret that she wanted him to view her not as an up-and-coming assistant, but as a wealthy graduate of Cornell University who had set her cap not so much on an illustrious career in the D.A.'s office as on the A.D.A.—seeing as how the D.A. was taken. To Marcia it was all about connections.

"Woods wants us all in the conference room," she

told Janelle. Belatedly, she seemed to take note of the fact that Janelle was not alone. "Well, hello," she declared with more than a little feeling.

Marcia's normally frosty delivery had warmed up several degrees. Obviously Sawyer brought out the best in someone, if not herself, Janelle thought. Marcia usually behaved as if she were entering a leper colony every time their paths crossed. The woman considered her an unworthy rival. Her dark eyes quickly swept over Sawyer's impressive torso, coming to rest on the holster he wore. She rubbed her thumb over her fingers, as if vicariously feeling the leather.

"Packing heat, I see," Marcia murmured appreciatively, raising her eyes to his. Her mouth curved. "And you have a gun, too."

Janelle looked at Sawyer. His expression was unreadable. But if he was a typical male, she thought, he was probably eating this all up.

"Here's a thought, why don't you guard *her* body?" Janelle suggested. Not waiting for a response or comment, she grabbed her portable notebook and darted around Marcia as if she were a mere obstacle to be circumvented.

The latter smoothly shifted in order to block Sawyer's exit. "Why don't you?" she purred, looking up at him.

"Yours wasn't the name I was given," Sawyer replied simply. In no mood to exchange banter, he took hold of Marcia's shoulders and physically moved the assistant to the side.

"I won't tell if you won't tell," Marcia offered, raising

her voice to be heard. She'd said the words to his back as he quickly strode down the corridor.

With a careless shrug, Marcia hurried to catch up to Janelle.

The meeting—*briefing* would have probably been a more apt description for it—was called to let the four score and plus people who worked for the D.A.'s office in on what was going on and to explain the presence of both Sawyer and the other detective.

The situation necessitating his having a bodyguard would just be temporary, Woods assured them. In response, Marcia made a small, disappointed sound, like a kitten anticipating being left out in the snow without food. The noise was audible only to the handful around her. But it included Janelle and Sawyer.

Janelle slanted at look toward him. It was her turn to smirk and she enjoyed it. "Well, it looks like you have a groupie."

"A what?"

"A groupie," she repeated. When there was no indication that he knew what she was talking about, she couldn't help staring at him. "Don't you know what a groupie is?"

He had a tendency not to retain things if they didn't have a direct bearing on his work. "Not really, but I have a feeling I'm not going to like it."

"A fan," Janelle explained. "An *intense* fan. Usually female. You can track her by following the drool marks on the ground." She paused for a moment, then put it in more familiar terms. "In a parallel universe, you might think of a groupie as a stalker."

He snorted. "I don't believe in a parallel universe," he told her. "There's too much garbage to deal with in this one."

He had that right, she thought. And part of that garbage was standing right behind her in the conference room. It made her nostalgic for the "good old days" when all she'd had to contend with was an overwhelming workload.

There was more to the briefing than just the necessary introductions and a summary of events that had brought about the detectives' presence in the D.A.'s office. Verbal progress reports were given. The various assistants discussed how far along they were in their individual cases and whether or not there was enough to indict the defendants.

Janelle found she had difficulty keeping her mind on the subject even though she was concentrating as hard as she could. She felt as if her thoughts were leaning in two different directions. Part of her mind was still on Wayne and the phone call. Although she hated to admit that Sawyer was right, the crime lieutenant could have compromised her position in the case just by calling.

Thinking, she chewed on her lower lip. Should she tell Woods, or take a risk that Sawyer would keep his mouth shut about this? After all, it wasn't as if Wayne had offered her a bribe, or even hinted at one. And she certainly hadn't done anything improper—other than not immediately hang up on him. Sawyer had taken care of that, she thought darkly.

What if Wayne had taped their conversation? she thought suddenly. He could have the tape altered, make it sound as if she'd said something she hadn't. If he did that, he could get a mistrial. And she'd be out on her ear.

She needed advice, Janelle thought.

There was only one person she went to openly for advise. Her father. She decided to go see him tonight, even if just to use him as a sounding board. Maybe, if she was lucky, he could help her get this damn monkey off her back.

Which brought her to the other reason that her mind kept wandering. She was having a devil of a time concentrating. Knowing that Sawyer was standing right behind her chair for some reason kept her mind from moving forward. From taking in more than a few sound bites at a time as the A.D.A., or someone else at the conference table, was speaking. Part of the reason, she supposed, was that she was waiting for a sneak attack, the way she used to when she was a kid and one of her cousins or brothers was out to get her at any time, any place.

She had no idea why that feeling seemed so pertinent now.

Sawyer wasn't here to attack her, she silently argued, he was here to protect her from an attack. While antagonizing her at every turn. Was that on purpose? Was he doing that to keep her at a distance?

That was it, she realized suddenly. Sawyer was being surly and off-putting to assure himself that she would remain at arm's distance. That she wouldn't get to know him, break through his steel reserve. For some reason, that seemed to bother him.

The good thing about having so many male relatives milling around, she thought, her mouth curving, was that the mystery of the male psyche was pretty much exposed to the light of day.

She glanced smugly over her shoulder toward her shadow just as Woods was winding up the impromptu meeting.

I have your number, Detective Sawyer Boone. And I'm pretty sure that I know how to use it.

Chapter 5

Janelle glanced at her watch. She'd been at this a number of hours now. Since her office had no windows, she couldn't identify the portion of the day by the sun's position in the sky. But she could congratulate herself for being able, for the most part, to block out the man seated to the side. Pausing, she looked at him now. Sawyer was reading some paperback book he'd pulled out of his jacket earlier.

Probably something triple-X-rated, judging by the way it absorbed him, she mused. Tired, not making nearly enough headway, Janelle dropped her pen and rocked back in her chair, careful not to lean too far. The chair was somewhat unstable.

Sawyer seemed oblivious to his surroundings. Some

bodyguard. "So, just what's the plan here? You're going to sit there all day, reading, while I work?"

He glanced over in her direction. Nothing had escaped him since they'd entered this oversize crayon box of a room. Ever on the alert without giving that impression, a burst of adrenaline was only half a heartbeat away.

Still, he managed to sound almost lazy as he said, "Pretty much."

She would have thought a man like him would be going stir-crazy by now. But then it occurred to her that everything she knew about him was just supposition on her part. Beyond what her brother had mentioned earlier, no one had given her Sawyer's credentials. Something she was going to have to look into the first chance she got, Janelle promised herself.

Until then, she went on instinct, picturing one of her brothers in this same situation. "Doesn't that bother you?"

Since the conversation didn't appear to be ending, he closed the book he was reading, marking his place with his index finger. His eyes swept over her. "You have no idea."

She leaned forward a little, wanting suddenly to distract him. "Then why didn't you protest?"

He lifted one wide shoulder in a careless, dismissive manner. As far as battles went, his were chosen carefully. And they had already had this conversation. "I did. It wouldn't do any good."

"You don't strike me as the kind of man who just goes along with the flow. More like someone who swims upstream, defying gravity and tides."

Her words evoked something akin to a smile. Whether it was at her expense or just amusement, she couldn't quite say. "If you're trying to flatter me into going away, it won't work. You're my assignment," he told her stoically, "until I get liberated."

"So guarding me is your idea of being in prison."

He regarded her for a long moment. "Pretty much."

Janelle felt that she'd just caught him in a contradiction. A feeling of satisfaction began to bubble up inside of her.

"You threw yourself over me in front of the courthouse," she pointed out. If he had no desire to protect her, why had he risked his life then?

He looked unfazed, and she felt satisfaction slipping away. "That was different."

Janelle tried to make sense of the man. "Why? Because no one told you to do it?" That kind of a feeling was the stuff action movies were made of. Real life, however, was different. "You draw a paycheck, Detective, you follow rules."

She saw his eyes pass over her again. Slowly. So slowly that she could almost feel them as they passed. Feel them assessing her. Touching her. She found it hard not to squirm.

"You follow rules?" he asked, his voice close to expressionless.

"Whenever possible." Okay, it was a lie, but he didn't have to know that. But the look on his face told her he didn't believe her simple statement. It rankled her even though he was right, or maybe because he was right. She didn't want him to feel as if he were privy to secret information about her.

Janelle followed rules when she felt they were right, or when she had no other choice. But there was a whole gray area that came up between those two points, an area where rules were bent when they needed to be—and when she felt she could get away with it. The trouble was, she believed in honor and justice, but there were times when the two turned out to be mutually exclusive. And then her choice was clear.

Sawyer was still studying her face. "Define possible."

It was a challenge. How did this man manage to get under her skin so fast, especially when she'd been so confident that she could handle him? That she had his number and could put him in his place?

Obviously, she was wrong.

She sighed. This was going nowhere. "I'd love to continue this philosophical conversation with you, Detective Boone, but one of us has work to do and it's obviously not you."

If she meant the last as a little dig, it didn't get the desired results. Sawyer gestured toward her desk, indicating that she was free to get back to what she was doing. "Didn't mean to keep you from it."

The hell he didn't, she thought. This man was angry, angry that he'd been ordered over here, to watch over her instead of doing whatever it was he normally did. And he was taking it out on the only person within firing range. Her.

She didn't have the time to get distracted. Or to

engage in some kind of mental duel. Swallowing an impatient sigh, she lowered her head and looked back at the three open reference volumes spread out before her. With effort, she blocked Sawyer out and resumed trying to find cases that would back up the points of law that she felt would be raised during the trial.

At times, the law was nothing more than a big chess game. It wasn't about right and wrong so much as about thinking three moves ahead. About being able to outwit your opponent and block legal moves, like motions to suppress evidence that could clearly win the case for them if it was admitted. Justice and truth had a way of getting lost amid the logistics sometimes.

That was the part she hated about the legal system. That in protecting the rights of hypothetical citizens, criminals got off free and victims had no recourse, no feeling of being championed and vindicated. It was all for the ultimate greater good, but it certainly didn't feel that way. Especially not to the victim or the victim's family.

Janelle heard Sawyer shifting in his chair. She refused to look up, refused to let her thoughts stray in that direction.

She did her very best to concentrate on the case and shut out the very real, very distracting presence of her temporary bodyguard. The faster this case was resolved, the faster she would be allowed to cast her own shadow and not have someone provide it for her.

Despite her resolve, ignoring Detective Sawyer Boone was not easy. She only hoped that he wasn't aware of just how "not easy" it was.

* * *

The crick was becoming worse. Raising her hand, Janelle spread her fingers out along the back of her neck and began to massage muscles that could have doubled as rocks. Still massaging, she rotated her head from side to side.

Time to call it a day, she thought. There was nothing to be gained by pushing when she felt this tired. Besides, she wanted to drop in on her father at a decent hour for a change.

When she felt hands suddenly on her shoulders, she immediately stiffened. Janelle tried to turn, but those same hands wouldn't allow it. They held her firmly in place.

Sawyer had vacated his seat and was directly behind her.

"What do you think you're doing?" she demanded.

Sawyer didn't answer her immediately. When he finally did, it wasn't a reply to her question. She was beginning to notice that her bodyguard had a nasty habit of never answering anything directly. He responded either with a question of his own or employed some sort of sideways logic. Like now.

"Nobody can give themselves a proper massage," he told her matter-of-factly as he kneaded the knots along both sides of her neck.

Pain shot through the top of her head and fanned out along her shoulders, making its way down through her chest. The only part of her upper torso left unaffected was her waist.

Mercenaries probably tortured their enemies this

way, Janelle thought. It was hard for her to take in a complete breath.

"And you've made a study of this?" she asked with effort, gritting her teeth together to keep from moaning out loud in pain. Maybe it was childish, but she refused to give him the satisfaction of letting him know that this was hurting.

This time he responded with a question. "You always sarcastic?"

"Only…when…I'm being…tortured." Was it her imagination, or did he just increase the pressure he was exerting? Each of his fingers felt as if it was forming a hole in her neck. She bit the inside of her lip to keep from wincing.

"This isn't torture," he told her, sounding almost cheerful. "I promise, you'll know when I'm torturing you."

"Not something I intend to find out," she retorted. Shifting suddenly, she managed to surprise him and momentarily elude his grasp. Janelle was on her feet in less than a heartbeat, just in case he had any ideas of continuing to squeeze her shoulders with his hamlike pincers.

As the throbbing slowly faded away, so did the initial pain that had prompted her to begin the massage in the first place.

Coming around in front of her, Sawyer lowered his head until his eyes were level with hers. He put the question to her mildly.

"Better?" The expression on his face told her that she already had his answer and was only going through the motions to be polite.

"Better," she allowed grudgingly.

Swiftly shutting down her computer, she butted her chair up against the desk and took out her purse. Out of the corner of her eye, she saw Sawyer pick up his jacket from the back of his chair, stuff the paperback book he'd been reading into one of the pockets and fall into step with her. She still wasn't able to catch the title, but the front page didn't appear too colorful.

"Walking me to my car?" she asked as she went down the corridor to the elevator.

"And places beyond," he added.

Janelle stopped abruptly in front of the elevator. An uneasiness wafted over her as she punched the down button. She hadn't thought about this part. Hadn't thought about anything except how annoying it was to have this man assigned to following her around all day while she was at work. She had no doubts if she'd gone out for lunch instead of ordered in, Sawyer would have been right there beside her in the restaurant.

But for some reason, she had just assumed that when her workday ended, the detective would just fade into the woodwork.

He wasn't fading.

"What parts?" she asked, more than a hint of suspicion in her voice. *Please don't say what I think you're going to say.*

Prayers weren't always answered in the affirmative. She'd learned that long ago, but didn't particularly like having it reaffirmed now.

"I'm supposed to go wherever you go."

The elevator car arrived, its silver doors opening wide. Janelle stepped inside, never taking her eyes off him.

"And what?" she demanded heatedly. "You're going to guard me 24-7?"

"That's the deal."

"How?" she asked, her voice rising since it was just the two of them in the elevator. "What are you, a robot? Don't you sleep?"

He took no exception to her irritated tone. He didn't have to. Although he didn't want this assignment, he liked being told to get off it even less. "Don't need much."

Janelle nodded, taking his words in as if they were gospel. "Just an occasional can of oil," she assumed sarcastically.

He didn't so much as blink an eye. "Not even that," he countered without cracking a smile.

This was really getting to be unacceptable, she thought. It was bad enough having him around all day. She refused to have him around after hours. "I'm going to go see my father."

"All right."

"Alone," she underscored.

The elevator was going straight down to the first floor without making any other stops. For all she knew, she was going straight down to hell. It certainly felt that way.

Sawyer retracted his approval. "Not all right."

As she turned toward him, her eyes were shooting daggers. He found it mildly diverting. "My father is the chief of detectives—"

The knowing expression on his face infuriated her. "Wondered when you'd get around to saying that to me. Just how much mileage do you figure you get off that little phrase, say, in a week's time?"

She wondered if there was any place in the basement where a body could be hidden. "We've had that conversation, Detective Boone. And frankly, it's getting a little old. *My point was,* he's the chief of detectives, and someone would have to be pretty stupid to try to hurt me while I'm with him. So you don't have to tag along," she concluded.

"In my experience, people in organized crime aren't generally card-carrying members of Mensa. They don't even have to have double-digit IQ. They just have to know how to take orders and that there are consequences if they don't carry them out."

Janelle pressed her lips together. She wasn't going to lose her temper, she wasn't. She would remain calm—even if it killed her. Although she would have much preferred that it killed him instead.

"Okay," she said as they walked out of the building. "You can come. But you'll stay in the car." She was going to stand firm on this point. What she had to say to her father was private and this walking annoyance was a stranger, even if he had been privy to the phone call she wanted to discuss with her father.

His expression gave nothing away. "As long as I get to crack a window."

"Are we going in my car?" Even as she asked, she braced herself for an answer she wasn't going to welcome.

But he surprised her. "I'll follow you in mine," he told her. "And if you're thinking of losing me," he added, "don't. I've tailed the best."

Just who exactly was this man? she wondered. Dax hadn't given her much to go on. She needed to talk to him, find out more. Better yet, maybe her father knew him. Her father was more likely to give her a straight answer. She'd ask him—once she talked to him about Wayne's phone call.

She walked ahead of Sawyer to her car. "So you say," she responded. She didn't look over her shoulder to see if that annoyed him, but she could hope.

She had ten miles. Ten miles in which to try to calm down. Ten miles in which to try to lose the source of her frustration.

Janelle did her best to accomplish both.

Ten miles turned out not to be enough. She failed miserably on the second count and succeeded only marginally on the first. Which ultimately didn't matter. As it turned out, she didn't need to be calm for her father's sake.

There were no lights on in her father's house when she pulled up in the driveway. At least, none coming from the inside of the house. There was a light on by the front door. Being the only handy one in the family, she and her father had spent one Saturday putting in an old-fashioned street lamp at the beginning of the walk. Her father had it set on an automatic timer. Five o'clock in the winter, seven o'clock in the summer.

It was after seven, and there was no indication that anyone was home.

Janelle tried anyway.

Getting out of the car, she went up the front walk. Behind her, she heard Sawyer pull up in his sports car. She looked over her shoulder and saw that he'd parked along the curb. The tail end of his car was over in the driveway just enough to block hers.

He'd done that on purpose, she thought. To make sure that she couldn't peel out once she was done. She didn't like the fact that he was one step ahead of her.

Janelle frowned as she approached the front door. Annoying as he was, right now, her mind wasn't on Sawyer, it was on the Wayne case. And on the fact that her father wasn't where she needed him to be. He couldn't still be at work. She'd called his office just before winding down and the assistant had told her that he'd left for the day.

She'd assumed that he'd left for home, as usual.

Like her siblings and her uncle, she had a key to the house. After ringing the doorbell once to give her father fair warning in case he was entertaining a lady friend— which would have been a first since none of them had been able to get her father to agree to even a single date with a woman—Janelle let herself in.

"Dad?" Despite the furnishings, her voice echoed as it penetrated the darkness. "Dad, are you home?" Turning on the light, she walked into the living room.

The second she did, Janelle was immediately aware of someone right behind her. She swung around, her fist raised defensively, ready to punch, gouge, whatever was necessary.

She muttered an unflattering oath as her fist was completely swallowed up by Sawyer's hand.

Sawyer pushed her hand down to her side. "Down, champ."

She was edgy. And with good reason. Having a body-guard around spooked her. "I thought you said you were staying in your car and cracking the windows."

"That was when you were going in to talk to your father." He gestured around the empty house. "There's no one home."

He made her want to prove him wrong. Desperately. "Dad?" Janelle raised her voice so that it could be heard on the second floor.

No response.

"Should have called ahead," Sawyer told her mildly. And then he paused for a moment, as if to gauge her thoughts. "Do you want to go check out the rooms upstairs?"

She absolutely *hated* that he kept second-guessing her this way. He didn't know her; how did he know what she wanted to do?

Without answering, she turned on her heel and headed toward the stairs.

"Dad?" Janelle called again, even louder this time. She still got the same response. Silence.

Stubbornly, she checked out the rooms on the second floor. They'd all moved out a while ago, but Brian Ca-vanaugh had left his children's rooms intact, in case they ever needed to stay over for some reason. She supposed in a way, it helped him cope with being alone after all these years.

Her father wasn't home. She caught her lower lip between her teeth. He *never* went out after work. Unless…

"Ready to go home?" Sawyer asked.

She didn't answer. Instead, she took out her cell phone and she pressed a familiar number. Someone on the other end picked up after two rings.

"Hello? Aunt Rose? This is Janelle. Is my father there?"

"Hi, Janelle," a warm voice responded. "He's right here. Do you want to speak with him?"

She shifted beneath Sawyer's gaze. This wasn't the time to go into anything, not while he was listening. "No, not right now, Aunt Rose. Just tell him I'll call him later tonight. Or tomorrow," she added, to take the urgency off. She didn't want anyone worrying.

"Does he know what it's about?"

"Probably." Janelle smiled to herself. "He knows everything." Or so he always told her and her brothers. For a long time, she'd believed him. "Bye." She shut her phone and slipped it back into her purse.

Sawyer was leaning against the wall opposite her, his hands in his pockets. His indolent pose didn't fool her for a moment. He was as alert as a rattler, ready to strike.

"Do you want to wait for him here?" Sawyer asked. "Or are you ready to go home?"

"Home," Janelle answered.

The minute the word was out of her mouth, she suddenly realized that *home,* her apartment, wasn't going to be the haven she'd come to regard it. Not if Sawyer was coming with her.

She raised her eyes to his. And knew. There was no talking him out of it. Under any circumstances.

Chapter 6

"You're coming home with me."

It wasn't a question so much as a shell-shocked statement. One that, Janelle hoped, if uttered out loud, would be summarily negated by the man leaning against the wall in front of her. She didn't *want* this man coming home with her. What would it take to make him go to his own place for the night and resume this little charade in the morning?

Sawyer straightened, moving away from the wall. Ready to leave. "If that's where your body's going."

How could such a flat, emotionless statement evoke anger, panic and a sense of invasion all in one fell swoop? She had no answer and that only made her feel more unsettled. Janelle juggled all three reactions, doing her best not to come across like a hysterical female, even though, if she were being honest with herself, she was very close to being just that.

She didn't want this man in her apartment. Wasn't putting up with him all day enough? She tried to reason with him despite the sinking feeling in her stomach that she was just wasting words. "Look, this is really above and beyond the call of duty—"

"This *is* duty. Don't worry, counselor, you won't even know I'm there."

"That's like saying a Tibetan monk doesn't know that the Himalayas are there."

Sawyer couldn't exactly say why, but he was enjoying this. Maybe it was a case of misery wanting company. He didn't know, then again, he was never much into analyzing things.

A hint of amusement was reflected in his eyes as he looked at her. "You saying I'm covered in snow?"

"No." *Not that I wouldn't want to bury you in it up to your neck.* "I'm saying that you're a little hard to miss."

He nodded, as if he were taking her comment under consideration. "I'll try harder to blend in."

The only way this man could "blend in" would be if she threw a slipcover over him and left him in the spare bedroom with the rest of the things to be dealt with at a later date. Periodically, she would go through the room and clean it out. Currently, however, it looked like the nesting ground for abandoned creatures who found shelter beneath bridges and inside collapsing cardboard boxes.

Fighting a sense of mounting desperation, Janelle

walked out of her father's house. She locked the front door and pocketed the key before finally looking at the man she now regarded as her own personal albatross.

"You don't have to come with me," she insisted. "I won't tell if you don't tell."

It didn't work that way for him. You weren't guilty only if you were caught. You were guilty if you did something wrong. Witnesses didn't count.

He looked at her for a long silent moment, wondering if she was just talking or if her moral foundation was built on lies. "But I'll know."

"And honor is that important to you."

"Shouldn't it be?"

Normally, yes, she thought. But not in this instance. "Terrific, I draw Dirty Harry with a conscience." Well, she might as well make the best of it, she supposed as she opened the driver's side door. "You can have the sofa."

Woman certainly jumped around from topic to topic, he thought. "To do what on?"

"Sleep."

Sawyer laughed shortly, shaking his head. "I don't intend to sleep."

Janelle stopped just short of getting into her car and stared at him. "You're kidding, right?" When he made no effort to confirm her supposition, she felt compelled to point out a glaring fact of life. "Everyone sleeps, Detective."

He'd been in the marines and seen fighting. He'd been an LAPD officer and seen more. Somewhere along the line, he'd developed the ability to sleep sitting up with one eye open. That way, he rested, but the slightest noise would instantly wake him up.

"If you say so."

His "agreeableness" was anything but. She didn't like his patronizing attitude. But she was too tired, too edgy, too stressed to debate this situation any further.

Taking one last look around the area to see if her father's cream-colored sedan was approaching, Janelle did her best to suppress her frustration and got behind the wheel of her car. She didn't even remember turning on the ignition. As far as she was concerned, it was all automatic pilot from door to door.

The roads were empty. She did sixty all the way. Sawyer kept up with her. He wasn't that far behind her when they pulled up into her apartment complex. Janelle drove straight into her carport without so much as a backward glance in her rearview mirror, leaving her shadow to find a space in guest parking if he could. What with many of the apartments having at least two occupants if not more, this time of the evening there were usually very few empty spaces to be found.

His problem, not mine, she thought.

Maybe if he couldn't find a place to park, he'd go away. At least it was something to hope for.

For a very short time.

Sawyer was only two steps behind her when she reached her front door. She pressed her lips together to keep from ordering him home. It wouldn't accomplish anything, except make her unstable. She was determined not to appear weak around him.

Inserting the key into the lock, she opened the door and entered.

"You know, you could have gotten a ticket back there."

Her voice was heavy with sarcasm. "Lucky for me there were no dedicated police officers around."

She switched on the light in her apartment. For the first time she found herself wishing that she'd listened to her father when he'd suggested she get an attack dog after she'd first moved out. Her reasoning against it had been that she didn't have enough time to properly take care of a pet. But right now, she would have loved to see Sawyer's reaction if a snarling dog came lunging at him.

He'd probably shoot it, she realized suddenly. The man struck her as the type to shoot first, ask questions later.

Brooding about this wasn't going to help. If life threw lemons at you, you made lemonade, right? She'd get through this, she promised herself.

Taking in a deep breath, she tossed her purse down on a nearby chair.

"You hungry?" she asked as she crossed to the refrigerator. Opening it, Janelle found herself looking at empty rack space. She hadn't had time to go shopping for food and nothing had magically appeared on her shelves.

Her mouth twisted in a fond smile. Every so often, Uncle Andrew, dabbling in what amounted to his third passion, right after his family and law enforcement, would experiment with a new recipe and leave a sample of whatever he'd created in her refrigerator. He, along with her father and siblings, had a key to her place. She was the only unattached Cavanaugh and as such, had no one to help her out. No one to fill an empty refrigerator.

Obviously, if Uncle Andrew was experimenting, he and Aunt Rose were consuming whatever it was he was creating.

"I could eat," Sawyer allowed. Coming up behind her, Sawyer looked into the interior of the refrigerator. "Invisible food?" he guessed.

He was mocking her, she thought, struggling with a flash of temper. She was also struggling with another unsettling feeling. An unwelcome warmth spread through her. The man was standing too close for her comfort.

Janelle swung the refrigerator door shut a little too hard. "I was thinking of ordering takeout. Chinese? Pizza?"

To her relief—and suspicion—he'd left her side and the kitchen. "Didn't know the Chinese made pizza."

Very slowly, Sawyer looked around, absorbing the lay of the apartment. Moving like a panther that was ready to pounce on a stalking enemy in less than a heartbeat, the detective went from room to room, making sure they were all empty and free of any surveillance equipment. The pretty woman in the other room struck him as a tad naive, especially considering her family background.

"Whatever," he tossed in as an afterthought.

Janelle frowned at the careless answer. She'd asked him for a reason. To make a choice. *Whatever* was not a choice. It would, however, probably give him a chance to complain about whatever it was she did select.

"How about cattle feed?" she asked sarcastically.

Sawyer raised what was almost a perfectly shaped eyebrow as he looked at her over his shoulder. "Didn't take you for someone whose tastes ran in those directions."

Enough was enough, she thought. She was hungry and she wanted to eat. Before morning came. "Pizza," Janelle declared.

His shrug was vague and noncommittal. Sawyer didn't care what she wound up ordering. It wouldn't have been what he wanted anyway. Because tonight, in hopes of at least slightly appeasing his hunger, he found himself craving a whiskey, neat.

Several shots, actually. Something to drown out, or at least tone down, the presence of this woman he was supposed to be guarding. But the very fact that he was guarding her dictated that he consume nothing stronger than a double shot of espresso.

He needed a clear head.

God knew that being around Janelle Cavanaugh and her smart mouth wasn't conducive to having a clear head. Between her antagonistic nature, which both amused and galled him, and that perfume she was wearing that softly announced her presence moments before she was actually there, he felt as if his head were submerged in seawater.

There was irony for you, he mused. Her perfume subtly announced what her tongue loudly proclaimed. In his book, she didn't need the perfume—or the chip on her shoulder for that matter.

Even if she just stood still, a person couldn't help

noticing her. There was just something about the woman that caught a man's attention, that fired his imagination. He wished that weren't the case. He wished that Janelle Cavanaugh was colorless enough and mousy enough to fade into any gathering of two or more. His job would be a hell of a lot easier. In a lot of ways.

But then, he did like a challenge and she was that. Right from the word *go*. Just being around the woman without telling her exactly what he thought of her and her damn superior attitude came under the heading of one hell of a challenge.

"Your apartment's clear," he told her, walking back into the kitchen.

Janelle saw him holstering his weapon. All of her brothers wore holsters and guns beneath their jackets, as did her cousins. She was accustomed to this and hardly noticed.

Except for now.

There was something incredibly masculine about the way Sawyer moved, the way he took charge.

Her sense of wonder warred with her sense of independence and her resistance to having him take over. This was *not* going to be an easy association, she thought as she hung up the receiver. Pizza was on its way. She'd selected the toppings of her choice since he hadn't voiced a preference. If Sawyer didn't like them, he was just going to have to deal with it.

Janelle looked at him meaningfully. They had a difference of opinion there, she thought. He might regard the apartment as clear, but she certainly didn't.

"No, it's not."

With that, she turned on her heel to go find Batman some bedding in case he was lying about his having no need to sleep.

The pizza box, its bottom shiny with the oils that had leeched out of their dinner, was empty.

Janelle reached for a napkin, wiping her lips and then her fingers before balling the paper up and tossing it into the box. She eyed Sawyer sitting across from her at the small, dinette-sized kitchen table. For once, his eyes weren't on her.

For a man who had expressed no desire to eat, he'd certainly done justice to the supersize pepperoni, sausage and cheese pizza she'd ordered. She'd hoped to have at least one slice leftover for breakfast, but that was no longer a possibility. He was consuming the last piece.

She supposed she couldn't really say anything about it, seeing as how he'd been the one to go to the door when the doorbell had rung—had insisted on it, actually and then had paid the delivery boy for the pizza.

When she'd tried to reimburse him, he'd abruptly cut her dead with that cold, distant voice of his. She supposed he was good at that, cutting people dead. With or without a look.

"Kill many people?" she heard herself asking out of the blue.

She was more surprised by her question than he was. Actually, he looked rather unfazed by it. In the background, one of the many forensic shows that littered the airwaves played on her thirty-inch TV. She had a weakness for the shows, for problems that were neatly solved in an hour, counting commercials. She wished life could imitate art.

Sawyer took his time answering. "Depends on what you mean by many."

Yup, the man was definitely dangerous. The minute she got into her bedroom for the night, she was going to pull out her laptop and see if she could access any information on her surly guardian angel. If that didn't yield anything, she was going to start pulling in some minor favors. Or lean on Brenda. Her brother Dax's wife was a wizard when it came to finding information.

"More than one?" she guessed, watching his profile.

The rigid contours gave nothing away. "Yes."

"Less than a hundred."

This time, he did raise his eyes. And just the slightest trace of a vein twitched for a second along his cheek. It almost succeeded in drawing her attention away from the hint of a smile on his lips. "Yes."

Well, that certainly left them a broad range. She'd only been kidding about the upper number. Now she wasn't all that sure. She could feel a shiver shimmying up her spine.

"Do you *know* how many?"

His eyes were flat. "Yes."

Janelle blew out a breath slowly. The man really *was* Dirty Harry. At least as far as the communication part went, she amended. Dirty Harry with a slice of Batman thrown in. Both fictional characters were portrayed as intense and humorless. And damn near monosyllabic. She was accustomed to far more talkative people. Even strangers she'd encountered talked more to her than Sawyer did.

"What does it take to get a conversation out of you?" she wanted to know. She half expected Sawyer not to answer.

Taking the last napkin, he wiped his hands, then tossed it on top of hers. "Something worth talking about."

Point and counterpoint.

Janelle stuffed both plates on top of the napkins, then closed the pizza-box lid. Getting up, she set the box aside on the kitchen counter. When she turned around, she saw that Sawyer had gotten up as well, an empty soda can in either hand. He put them on top of the pizza box.

"Okay," Janelle began gamely, picking up on his comment regarding worthwhile conversation, "tell me about yourself."

When he said nothing, she watched him expectantly. Had she not been staring, the movement of his head from side to side would have been imperceptible. "Not worth talking about."

"Modesty?" she asked.

"Fact," he stated flatly.

He might have no say in the assignment he was given, but no way was he about to let this person elbow her way into his private life. His private life was going to remain just that, private. No one else's business.

She studied his face as she spoke. "Everyone's life is worth talking about, Sawyer."

Just his luck to be told to guard a woman who could talk the ears off a stone statue. "It's getting late," he told her. "Maybe we should call it a day."

There were a few other things she wanted to call it—and him—but she kept that to herself.

She glanced over toward the television set. The program had ended without her noticing or finding out who was behind the murders. The eleven o'clock news with its barrage of depressing sound bites was just announcing the main headlines. While programs that dealt with solving crimes captured her interest, the news did not. There was too much sadness in the world for her to actively seek out more. Fiction she enjoyed. Reality was another matter.

Crossing over to the television set, she was about to shut it off only to have the picture suddenly fade into nothingness before her outstretched hand. She turned around behind her to see that Sawyer was holding the remote. He was aiming it at the set.

Typical male.

And yet, not so typical, really. At least, not when she compared him to the men in her family. Of course, her cousin Teri was married to Hawk, another detective on the Aurora police force. To say that the man had come across as less than a ray of sunshine when he'd originally hooked up with her cousin was a vast understatement.

Inside of every dark soul was a bit of sunshine, she thought. You just had to work the mine until you finally found it.

Janelle shoved her hands into the back pockets of her

jeans and took a defensive stance. Why did she even care if this man she was forced to put up with in her apartment even *had* a ray of sunshine inside of him? It made no different to her one way or another. He was just the thorn in her side right now, nothing more.

A temporary thorn, she underscored silently. Once the case was wrapped up, the powers that be were going to pull this thorn out and she would be alone again. Away from electric-blue eyes that seemed to penetrate her very skin and look right into her. Away from a man who made her feel unsettled and nervous and who seemed to be going out of his way to irritate the hell out of her.

She couldn't wait.

Chapter 7

Janelle punched her pillow for the umpteenth time. Defeated, the pillow could no longer rise to the occasion but lay there, as flat as her attempts to find slumber, or even some semblance of rest.

This wasn't going to work. If she didn't find a way around this situation, or how to at least tolerate it, she was going to wind up being a zombie by the time she had to show up in court.

Glancing to the side, she looked at the clock on her nightstand. The electric red numbers told her it was three minutes past two.

Janelle groaned.

Normally able to instantly fall sleep, she'd been tossing and turning since she'd slipped in between the sheets at midnight. All because there was a man, an unwanted man, in her living room, supposedly sitting guard.

A man about whom there was surprisingly little information available. She'd turned in at eleven and then had spent the next hour on her computer, hooking up into all the standard programs available to her and finding next to nothing. Name, rank and employee number, that was the extent of it. That and the fact that he'd been in the marines, then on the L.A. police force. She didn't even know where he was born.

Or if, she added sarcastically. For the most part, the man behaved like a robot.

How could there be no history of him? she wondered, frustrated. It was the same question that pulsed through her brain now. With the same answer. She hadn't a clue.

After shutting down her computer, she'd put in a call to Brenda. She'd asked for help once she'd apologized for having woken her up. Brenda had promised her that if there was anything to find, she'd find it. Janelle had hung up the phone thinking how nice it was that all her brothers had found women to share their lives with who were utterly likeable. There were families that splintered after siblings got married. Hers just grew closer together.

That thought and the fact that she might get information about her mysterious man-with-no-history bodyguard heartened her. For a few minutes.

But hope was slowly eroded as the darkness of night stained its fabric.

Not that she expected Brenda to call back within the hour. That was absurd. But her own inability to find anything had made her begin to think that maybe there was nothing to find. Which meant she was dealing with someone whose background had been covered up for some reason. Which led her to the question: Why?

She was getting punchy. Punchy and edgy and just this side of slightly irrational. And lying here like this was only going to get her more so.

Throwing back the covers, she sat up and swung her legs over the side. There were reference books in the bookcase in the other room that might be helpful with the Wayne case. No sense in just lying here, doing a bad imitation of a spinning top. She might as well do something useful with this downtime.

She didn't bother with the slippers at the foot of the bed. After grabbing her robe out of her closet, Janelle slipped it on and opened the door. From where she stood, she could see the back of Sawyer's head. He was sitting, not lying, on the sofa.

That didn't mean he wasn't asleep, Janelle thought. Plenty of people dozed off sitting up. She'd even fallen asleep once paging through a legal brief. But then, the kind of language that was found in a legal brief did not exactly make for scintillating reading.

Very softly, still watching the back of Sawyer's head, she made her way to the other room.

She was only three steps closer when Sawyer turned his head in her direction. She felt her heart sink. The man *was* a robot. With super hearing. She'd even been holding her breath.

"Going somewhere?"

"Sleepwalking," she countered.

He nodded, as if that were a perfectly plausible explanation for her moving around in the middle of the night.

"As long as I know," he murmured, going back to reading his book.

Curiosity got the better of her. She drew closer to try to see what was written on the cover. "What is it you're reading?"

His fingers were spaced so that they completely blotted out the title and author on the worn cover. "A book."

There wasn't enough light to make anything out. He'd shut off all the lights except the one on the side table and he'd turned that down to the lowest wattage. The scene might have even been construed as romantic, if Sawyer hadn't been the one on the sofa.

"I can see that," she retorted evenly. "What kind of book?"

"A good one."

His picture had to be in the dictionary, under infuriating. "Are you doing this on purpose to annoy me," she asked, "or does being a wiseass just come naturally to you?"

When she took another step closer, Sawyer half rolled up his book like a fat magazine and stuffed it into his back pocket.

"It's still early," he told her, changing the subject. "Why don't you go back to bed?"

Her eyes narrowed. Even as a kid, she hadn't liked being told what to do. And that was by people who had a right to do it. He didn't.

"If I wanted a recommendation or your opinion on the matter, I would have asked for it." Her statement would have sounded more forceful without the yawn that insisted on pushing its way in at the last moment. She blinked, focusing in on the kitchen. Her coffee-maker sat on the counter, dormant. If she was going to read—and make sense of what she was reading—she needed caffeine. "You want coffee?"

He considered her question for a moment. "I could stand to drink a cup."

"Good, so could I. Go make it," she instructed glibly. "The filters are in the cupboard just above the coffee-maker." She pointed toward it for his benefit. "I keep the coffee inside the refrigerator door."

She'd tricked him. Sawyer was about to say as much, but then stopped before the words had a chance to form. She'd caught him fair and square, he thought grudgingly, turned his own words around and used them against him. What was she like when it really counted?

The woman was probably hell on wheels in a courtroom, he judged. Maybe he'd watch her in action sometime. It'd be nice to see someone else on the receiving end of that smart mouth of hers.

But that was for later. Right now, he thought as he got up from the sofa, he had a couple of cups of coffee to make.

The scent of coffee, deep, rich, filled the predawn air and wafted into the room where Janelle was sitting, breaking up what could be best described as her extremely frail train of thought. There was just something almost sensual about sipping that first cup of coffee in the morning, having it seduce her senses.

Rousing herself, Janelle cocked her head, listening. Straining to hear.

But there was nothing to hear. No sound of someone approaching.

The man probably moved like a stealth bomber and was proud of it. Nevertheless, Janelle decided to get up and investigate.

Sawyer was back sitting on the sofa, a mug in one hand, his mysterious book in the other. He didn't even glance in her direction when she planted herself right in front of him, the backs of her calves hitting the coffee table. "I thought I asked you to make coffee."

"You did. I did," he said, the simple sentences echoing rhythmically like the staccato beat of high heels resounding against tile. Sawyer briefly raised his eyes from the book. "You didn't ask me to bring it to you," he pointed out.

"Next time I'll try to be clearer," she muttered under her breath as she moved toward the kitchen and the coffeepot.

"You do that." He hid a smile as he lowered his eyes back to the page he was reading.

Janelle's muttering continued. So did his smile.

She went back to bed shortly after that, deciding to try to snatch at least a few hours of sleep before she had to go in. It didn't matter that she'd had the coffee, or that it was the type that could have been used to resurface a driveway. Coffee had never acted as a deterrent for her when it came to sleeping. It had no effect on her.

Just bodyguards camped out in her living room seemed to induce insomnia, she thought darkly before she fell into a fitful sleep.

When she woke up again, streams of daylight were pushing their way into her room.

She was late.

Janelle hit the floor running. She lost no time in getting ready, showering and dressing in just under twenty minutes. Making her bed took another two.

Fastening her second earring, Janelle opened the door leading out of her room. Sawyer wasn't on the sofa. For a moment, she thought that maybe she was alone, but then she saw him in the kitchen, making a fresh pot of coffee.

At least he's good for something.

He had on a different shirt, she suddenly realized. And, coming closer, she noticed that his hair was slightly damp. There was a bathroom in the spare bedroom. That would explain his damp hair, she thought, trying not to let her mind stray too far in that direction. But it didn't explain the shirt.

Taking the bread out of the refrigerator, she put two slices into the toaster and slid down the timer. "You go home during the night?"

The first drops of brew made their appearance in the clear coffeepot, accompanied by the usual sound effects. "No. Why?"

She glanced in his direction. Was it her imagination,

or was the material clinging to his torso? And why did that look so sexy? "The shirt, it's different."

"I keep a change of clothes in the car," he told her. Sawyer slipped the coffeepot out and poured its spare contents into the mug he'd used last night. "Several," he added.

She should have known. "Prepared," she acknowledged. "Like a Boy Scout."

Boy Scouts tended to group together. He was a loner. Always had been, except for a brief period of time. When Allison had been part of his life.

"Like a man who's liable to be sent off on assignment," he corrected.

On second thought, she decided, there was nothing Boy Scout–like about this man. Boy Scouts made you think of baseball, apple pie and Mom. Boy Scouts were generally harmless. *Harmless* was the last word she would have used to describe Sawyer Boone.

For a second she entertained the thought of dragging him off to breakfast at her uncle Andrew's house just to see his reaction. The door to her uncle's house was always open. Rain or shine, no matter what the occasion or lack thereof, every morning the man made breakfast for an army.

If everyone showed up—and her uncle liked nothing better—it was a scene out of a crowd controller's worst nightmare. But Uncle Andrew loved it. The more, the merrier. If she hadn't been lucky enough to have the father that she had, Uncle Andrew would have been her hero. As it stood, it was close to a tie.

The toast popped. Taking the two slices out, she put them on a plate and pushed it along the counter to Sawyer. He raised an eyebrow in acknowledgment and she nodded back.

"Margarine's in the refrigerator," she told him.

He picked up the top slice. "I take it dry."

"Of course you do." And at home, he probably slept on a bed of nails—when he slept, she amended.

She had a hunch that Sawyer would have felt out of place in her uncle's kitchen, at least initially. But Uncle Andrew had a way of making people come around. And if for some reason he couldn't, there was always someone present at the table who could. She wondered how long it would take to breathe some life into Sawyer.

Janelle slanted a glance at him as her own toast popped up. He looked like a hard nut to crack. Hard, but not impossible.

Might be interesting to experiment. But the next moment she dismissed the thought. Sawyer was nothing to her, other than annoyance. There was no reason to put her family through the ordeal of having to break in yet another surly man at the table.

Meetings and an unexpected development in one of her other cases kept Janelle from finding the time to pick up the phone and make good on her promise to call her father the next day. And the next. Before she realized it, more than a week had gone by.

Meanwhile, as she labored and juggled the cases she had on her desk, trying to give each as much time as she was able, she became aware of the fact that she was feeling progressively more claustrophobic. Because of Sawyer.

Not that he smothered her in rhetoric. If anything, he'd become even more quiet than before. During her long workday, marked by endless incoming calls, mountains of reference texts and a parade of nondescript fast food in overly greasy wrappers, she noticed that Sawyer just sat there, reading the bent, dog-eared book he kept shoved in his jacket pocket.

Even so, he gave her the impression that he could spring into action at less than a moment's notice. A coiled snake, ready to strike if there was a need. He was every bit the protector. But that didn't negate the fact that his very presence seemed to throw a heavy blanket over her very being, pressing her down until she felt almost flattened. And sealed off from the rest of the world.

She did her best to shake the feeling. When that didn't work, she tried to ignore it. It only became worse. Worse because she felt that if they truly butted heads, she would be sent flying. She didn't like feeling as if she were in second place. She hadn't tolerated it with her brothers and she wasn't going to tolerate it with Sawyer. But until the Wayne case was over, she was just going to have to make the best of it.

Pausing for a moment, she opened her drawer and took out a half-empty bottle of extra-strength aspirin. She screwed off the lid and shook out two tablets, then popped them into her mouth, swallowing without the benefit of water. She'd gotten good at that.

"Those things'll burn a hole in your stomach."

She could have sworn he was reading. Just went to show, he was watching her constantly. The claustrophobic feeling grew worse.

"They keep my head from falling off," she informed him.

"Whatever you say." He went back to reading.

She stared at him for a moment, at a loss for words if not emotions. Though he hid the title of the book he was reading, she could have sworn he was back at the beginning again. Was this some philosophical work of nonfiction that he subscribed to? A bible he read and reread, committing it to memory?

What the hell did she care what he read, so long as he read it away from her?

Not bloody likely, at least not any time soon, she thought moodily.

Unaccountably, her thoughts turned to the phone call she'd taken from Marco Wayne. She hadn't thought about it in days. Now that she did, the discomfort returned. Innocent of any wrongdoing, she still didn't feel right about keeping this to herself. The man had sounded sincere, but then, he'd probably perfected that, lying to the police and to prosecutors under oath.

Damn it, Marco Wayne wasn't innocent and neither was his son, but she was. No real information had been exchanged in that short conversation. All Marco had said was that he wanted what every father wanted, a fair trial for his son. His saying that Tony was framed was a feeble attempt at her sympathy, nothing more.

And it hadn't worked, she told herself. She didn't believe him, not really.

Her mind played devil's advocate, reminding her that even though the conversation had been innocent, things could still be said, scenarios misrepresented. Rumors planted.

She had to be sure she was on safe ground.

Ordinarily, she knew she should go to Woods and then Kleinmann in turn, but before she went through all that, she wanted advice from a friendlier source.

Backup, so to speak. Her mouth curved at the familiar police jargon that had popped into her head. There was no denying that she was a cop's daughter.

It was time for the cop's daughter to call her dad, she thought. Instead of using the landline, she took out her cell phone and pressed a single number.

"Roz? This is Janelle Cavanaugh. Is my father there?"

"For you? Always," the woman on the other line assured her. Roz Smith had been her father's assistant/secretary since he'd taken the position of chief of detectives eight years ago. "Just hang on a minute, let me go round him up."

Leaning back in her chair, Janelle drew in a long breath, then let it out. She was aware that Sawyer had raised his eyes from his book and was watching her even before she looked in his direction.

No doubt about it, the man made her feel naked and exposed. Maybe her father could take care of this problem, too. If she had to have a bodyguard, she wanted a man who truly did fade into the wallpaper, not who made every nerve ending in her body rise to the surface in anticipation of God only knew what.

The next moment, her father's rich baritone voice was filling her ear. "So how's my favorite daughter?"

Janelle grinned. She was his only daughter, a fact that she rather relished. "Still gorgeous," she bantered.

"That would be your mother's doing," Brian assured her.

"Really?" She pretended to be skeptical. There was no denying that she looked very much like her mother. She also looked a great deal like all her female cousins—save for Patience—blond, small-boned and petite. "I always thought my looks came from the Cavanaugh side."

"Can't argue that," he told her with a chuckle. "Not to rush you, honey, but I've a meeting to go to in ten minutes. Seems our illustrious mayor has some new idea about the patrolmen's retirement benefits that just doesn't sound as if it'll go over all that well with our boys in blue. What's on your mind?"

She didn't waste time. "I need to talk to you, Dad. About Marco Wayne."

There was silence on the other end. It lasted so long, she thought she'd lost the connection.

"Dad, are you still there?"

"I'm still here." The humor had left his voice. "What about him?"

She knew he was in a hurry, but she still wanted to give him a little background before she dropped this little tidbit on him. "I caught the case against his son, and—"

"You're the assistant A.D.A. on the Anthony Wayne case?"

She heard the note of surprise in her father's voice and put her own interpretation on it. "I know, I know, you'd think he'd want someone with more time on the team at his side. But maybe the man recognizes talent when he sees it," she quipped. "Anyway, when can we get together to talk? I dropped by your place last Tuesday, but you weren't there."

"I know." Every word out of his mouth was an effort. He'd thought, believed, hoped that the matter was dead. Just went to show, nothing was ever really over. "Aunt Rose gave me the message. I expected you to call me sooner."

"Yeah, well, so did I. But everything's just crazy around here, Dad. There just doesn't seem to be an end to the work. Someday, they'll find me buried under a landslide of case files." Probably soon, she thought. "How does getting together tonight after work sound? Just you, me and my shadow."

A hopeful note elbowed its way into his serious tone. "You have a man in your life?"

"Unfortunately, I do." She stretched her lips into a wide, phony smile as she looked at Sawyer. "Detective Sawyer Boone. The D.A. assigned him to guard my body." Again, there was no response on the other end of the line. Her father was overworked, she thought, suddenly feeling guilty about dumping on him like this. "Dad?"

"I'm here, Janelle." *And I should have been here for*

you a lot sooner. He hoped he wasn't going to wind up paying for that. "How does six o'clock sound? At our favorite restaurant."

"Perfect." She felt better already. Her father always had that effect on her.

He'd noted her recent absences at Andrew's table. "It'll probably the first decent meal you'll have in a month."

"I've been eating pizza pretty steadily," Janelle admitted.

"Knew it. Andrew's been asking after you, saying you haven't been coming around lately."

"I've been awfully busy."

"You should never be too busy for family, Janelle."

He sounded so serious. She wondered if there was something going on that she didn't know about. "Dad, is something wrong?"

"No. I'll see you later, honey."

But something was wrong, Brian thought as he hung up the receiver.

He was going to have to tell her.

He had the meeting with the mayor in less than a few minutes, but somehow, that didn't seem nearly as important to him now as it had just moments ago.

The day he'd been dreading for the last twenty-eight years had finally arrived.

In his time, Brian Cavanaugh had faced down homicidal criminals pointing their weapon at him, gone into the line of fire so many times he'd lost count. He'd done it all feeling a great deal calmer and more confident than he did right now.

His men always said he had nerves of steel. Those same nerves deserted him now. When he needed them most.

He was finally going to have to tell Janelle the truth. And he was more than a little afraid of the outcome.

Chapter 8

The restaurant was crowded. And, as always, rather dimly lit. Until this moment, Janelle hadn't really paid that much attention to the limited visibility at the Three Queens Restaurant. The atmosphere seemed perfect for a romantic encounter.

Janelle glanced at the man inches away from her elbow. The man who had crowded into her life and, as far as she knew, ran on batteries instead of sleep because she'd never caught him at the latter. She had no doubts that to Sawyer, this was probably a good place for a shooting, or, at the very least, a meeting between two parties who didn't want to be seen together. Having been surrounded by them all of her life, she knew how a cop's mind worked. Especially one who rarely, if ever, cracked a smile.

Her father had chosen this restaurant, she knew, because it had been her mother's favorite and whenever she and her father came to eat here, they both felt close to Susan Cavanaugh.

Janelle looked toward what had become her father's favorite booth. It was the one he reserved each and every time.

Brian Cavanaugh was already there. There was a drink before him on the table. She thought that rather odd because her father rarely drank anything stronger than a beer, except on special occasions. Raising her hand, she waved to him. He nodded in response.

"Why don't you get a drink at the bar?" she suggested to Sawyer. "I'll be right there." For his benefit, and because she was feeling magnanimous, she indicated where her father was sitting.

Sawyer swiftly scanned the surrounding area within striking distance of the booth, taking measure of everyone within the vicinity. "Can't. I'm on duty."

About to make her way to her father's booth, she stopped and looked at him. She did *not* want the man at the table with her. "Okay, have a peanut at the bar. There's nothing against nuts on duty, is there?"

His mouth curved ever so slightly as he eyed her. She had no idea why she thought that looked sexy, or why there was this minute tremor in her stomach. Probably had to do with the lack of food, Janelle assured herself.

"Run into them all the time," he told her.

Not wanting to keep her father waiting any longer than he already had, Janelle didn't bother answering.

Turning her back on Sawyer, she made her way over toward her father's table. He had a drink waiting for her. A whiskey sour. And there was a shrimp cocktail beside it. All the things she liked. Her father had always had an eye for detail, she thought affectionately.

"Hi, Dad, thanks for coming."

She kissed him before sitting down across from him in the booth. Her father's smile was strained. An uneasy premonition snaked its way up her spine. She thought of saying something flippant to forestall whatever was coming, but she liked to think of herself as her father's daughter. That meant meeting challenges head-on instead of shying away from them.

"What's wrong?" She spread her napkin out on her lap, then curled her fingers around the chunky glass in front of her.

Brian Cavanaugh ran a hand through salt-and-pepper hair that had once been as black as the inside of midnight. The wedding ring he couldn't seem to remove caught a flash of sparse light before retreating into the shadows.

"Janelle," he began, then abruptly stopped as fear took away his power of coherent speech.

She was a student of his face, of every nuance that came or went across what she'd always regarded as a kindly surface. As a kid, she could gauge just how much trouble she and her brothers were in by the way her father's mouth was set, the way his eyebrows drew together. His cheekbones became really prominent when he was especially angry. They weren't prominent now, but whatever was on his mind had him really worried.

When he said nothing beyond her name, she felt her stomach tightening into a large knot. "Dad, you're scaring me."

He thought of taking another sip of his drink. But that was cowardly. Just as not facing this years ago had been cowardly. But he had wanted to protect her. Protect her and protect Susan. And now, matters had taken this out of his hands. He hated not being in control.

"Janelle," he began again. "You have to recuse yourself from the case."

The case. She almost felt giddy with relief. There wasn't anything wrong, her father was just overreacting to the threats. He was just being a dad. She could deal with that. And he was just going to have to deal with her being in the D.A.'s office.

"You had me worried there for a second." Taking one of the prawns that hung over the side of the frosted goblet, she popped it into her mouth without bothering to dip it into the sauce. It felt good to get something, however small, into her stomach. She couldn't remember eating lunch. "Dad, I can't just turn and run because someone fired shots outside the courthouse that might or might not have had anything to do with the Wayne case." His expression remained unchanged. She wasn't winning him over. "We've built a solid case. I've worked hard working up the background for this, I've been researching cases, we can—"

"You can't," Brian cut in.

He sounded so final, she thought. So abrupt. And he wasn't giving her a chance to state her side. This wasn't like him. She could always reason with her father. "What? Why?"

This was his fault. The facts only became harder to face with each passing year. "Because if the defense finds out," he said bluntly, "the case could get thrown out of court."

Damn it, how had *he* found out? "You're talking about the phone call," she assumed.

Her temper immediately flared. Sawyer was the only other person, besides Marco, who knew about the call that the crime lieutenant had made to her. Had Sawyer given her up to her father? Why? To make his job easier? To get rid of her as an assignment?

She turned and sought out her bodyguard, scanning the people lined up along the bar. Finding him was not a difficult matter. The man had a way of standing out in a crowd, rather than blending in. She imagined he probably found that annoying. As annoying as she found him right now.

Sawyer was staring straight at her. She suppressed a few choice words that popped into her head and turned back to look at her father. Because she'd been raised to be fair, she asked before mentally castrating Sawyer, "How did you find out?"

Brian shook his head. "What phone call?"

Okay, now she was lost. If he didn't know about the phone call from Wayne, why was he behaving like this? Was he just being overprotective? She knew he worried, but until now, she would have said that he was good at keeping his concerns under control.

For his benefit, she went over the event. "Marco Wayne called my office. Called me," she corrected. "I know I should have hung up right away," she followed up quickly, before he could voice the same sentiments, "but I did talk to him."

Janelle saw anger rise in her father's eyes. She had never seen him look this angry. "What about?"

That seemed like an odd question, considering that she was part of the D.A.'s team trying Anthony Wayne's case. But pointing it out would only fan the flames of a fire whose origin she didn't quite grasp yet.

"About his son. He said that he wanted to make sure that Tony got a fair trial. He also said that Tony was innocent, that his son was being framed. You know, the usual."

No, Brian thought, not the usual. Not when it involved Marco Wayne and his daughter. He looked at her darkly. "You shouldn't have talked to him."

She didn't want a lecture, especially not here. This just *wasn't* like her father, she thought again. What was going on? Was there something more going on here than she was aware of? Was this personal?

"I know, I know, but it was just that for a minute, Marco sounded very sincere and I guess I was caught off guard."

A feeling of déjà vu passed over him. It was almost as if he were hearing Susan's voice instead of Janelle's. "Funny, your mother said almost exactly the same thing to me twenty-nine years ago."

Janelle stared at him, stunned by this unannounced,

unexpected piece of information. "Mom? Mom knew Marco Wayne?"

Brian regarded the amber liquid in his glass, seeing something else. Seeing his past. "We both did. The three of us grew up together. Same neighborhood. We weren't exactly friends." He raised his eyes to Janelle's. "More like rivals. Marco always had a thing for your mother. And he had more money to shower on her. And he had that sexy, sophisticated thing going for him." His lips twisted in an ironic smile. "I was surprised when she picked me over him."

"I wouldn't have been." She reached across the table, covering his hand with her own. Talk about their mother always made him sad, she thought. "It's a no-brainer. You're a hell of a lot more man than he could ever be." The worried expression remained on her father's face. "I'll be all right, Dad, I promise. I not only have Neanderthal Man as my protector, but half the Aurora police force. And that's not counting you," she said, smiling at him warmly. "We all know what a difference you make."

He sat quietly for a moment, memorizing her smile. Absorbing it as he wondered if she would even forgive him for not having the courage to tell her years ago.

"Janelle," he finally said, "I have to tell you something."

She could feel nerves tap dance through her body. Her father wasn't given to melodrama. She braced, telling herself to think positively. "Okay."

Brian sighed. He would rather have faced an army of snipers than have to tell her this. Leaning forward, keeping his voice as low as he could and still be heard, he began.

"I should have told you this a long time ago, but the time never seemed right." There was another reason he'd held his peace. "Besides, it was your mother's secret to tell."

She could almost taste the metallic bite of fear along her tongue. "Go on."

He detoured for a moment. Perhaps the last moment he would ever have with her like this, he thought. "You know I love you, Janelle."

"Yes." Her eyes never left his face. "That's not where this is leading, Dad."

He tried again, aching for what was about to be lost. Trust. Innocence. A bond. "Your mother and I had a couple of rough patches."

She was aware that while her parents had loved one another, theirs was not exactly a storybook marriage. Her mother had been high-strung and, in the later years, given to depression, although she'd tried to keep it from her children. "Yes, I know."

"It wasn't easy for her," he continued, making excuses for the woman who no longer could defend herself. "She was a little anxious and I was working a really rough section of town then. She worried and we argued a lot about that. One thing led to another." He shrugged, not wanting to talk about the separation, that chasm that existed in their marriage right after the last of his sons had been born.

He paused, taking Janelle's hand in his. Mutely asking for her understanding. Her forgiveness for tearing down the image of her mother. For shaking her faith in him.

"I was hoping to never have to tell you," he admitted. "I didn't want you thinking any less of your mother."

Janelle was desperately trying to pull in the pieces so that they made some kind of sense, offered her a reason for her father's strange behavior. "So what are you going to tell me? That Mom had an affair with this Marco character?"

Even as she said it, she hated to think of her mother with anyone else other than her father. It shook the foundations of the happy family unit she had always wanted to believe existed. Her mother had had pockets of depression, pockets that had grown worse just before she'd died. Was this why? Because she'd felt guilty for having betrayed her husband and her vows?

"This is the twenty-first century, Dad," she pointed out, trying to cover up the disappointment she felt about her mother. "They don't attach the sins of the father to the sons, or sins of the mother to the daughter—"

As much as he wanted her to get sidetracked, he knew he had to see this through to the end. No more lies. No more hidden truths. "There's more."

The knot in her stomach grew larger, threatening to cut off her air supply. Janelle felt the roots of her hair tightening, tingling along her scalp.

"How much more?" And then, the reason behind her father's discomfort suddenly came to her. "Is Tony their son? Is that why Marco called me? Because Tony's my half brother?" Oh God, she thought, this was big. Very big. Her poor father—

As far as Brian knew, Marco didn't know the truth. Only he and Susan did. And Andrew. In a fit of despair, not knowing whether he could forgive Susan for what she'd done, he'd turned to Andrew for support. He'd gotten advice, as well. Advice to put the past behind him, reap only the good out of whatever presented itself before him and never look back.

Except now, even though it was against his will, he had to. "Tony's your half brother," he confirmed. "But he's not your mother's son."

Now he was talking in riddles. "I don't understand." But even as the last word left her lips, she did. She suddenly understood.

And desperately didn't want to. Wanted more than anything in the world to be wrong.

She felt her eyes stinging as she fought against the truth. "You're not telling me—" she began hoarsely, then tried again. "You're not telling me that Marco Wayne is…is my…"

He didn't want to hear her say it. Didn't want the word *father* to leave her lips and be applied to anyone else. He'd earned the right to be the man she thought of when she said the name.

"You were mine from the moment you came into the world, Janelle," he told her, his voice so filled with emotion, he had to block it in order to talk. "Mine even before then. I was the first one you looked at, the first one to hold you. You were always my daughter," he insisted fiercely.

Everything went pitch-black as the noise in the restaurant swirled around her, echoing the rhythm of her throbbing brain. Janelle took a deep breath to keep from giving in to the darkness that beckoned to her, that threatened to swallow her up whole, offering comfort within its belly. Comfort along with oblivion.

"In name only," she whispered.

"In every way that counted," he countered. He was not going to lose her because of this, because of his own cowardice. He couldn't.

"Except for blood," she snapped back. She was numb and furious at the same time. Her mind raced around, trying to make sense of this. Trying to find an explanation she could cope with. "Why didn't you tell me? When I think of all the times I prattled on about how much I looked like you, how much I acted like you—" She finished because she felt like such an idiot. And so betrayed she couldn't even begin to put it into words. "Why didn't you ever tell me?" she demanded again. She stared at the man sitting opposite her. Who *was* this man she'd thought she knew so well. "Were you laughing at me? Was I being entertaining enough for you?"

"Damn it, Janelle, nobody was laughing at you. I just told you why I couldn't bring myself to say anything. Especially after I lost your mother. You were my daughter, I loved you—"

She didn't believe him. "How could you love me?" she demanded hotly. She shot to her feet, ready to run off. "How could you not be disgusted? Every time you looked at me, you saw the living proof of your wife's infidelity, her betrayal—"

Brian caught her hands in his before she could get away. "How could I not be disgusted?" he echoed. "Because every time I looked at you, I saw a little girl I loved. And I watched her grow up to be a young woman I was proud of—"

"A young woman you lied to—" Janelle insisted angrily, trying to work her way around the pain that was ripping her in half. She wasn't his daughter. The man she adored, the man who was her key to a huge family network, to the people she had loved since forever, wasn't her father. She felt betrayed, alone. Lost. And angry. Oh, so very angry. At her mother, at this man she'd thought was her father. At Marco Wayne. And at herself for having to hear this.

Brian refused to release her hands, trying to hold on to the only bond he still had with his daughter.

She pulled her hands away from him, her heart breaking in too many places to count. Omitting something was the same as lying. "Damn it, Dad, or whatever I'm supposed to call you, you know better."

Just as with Susan that awful night she'd made her confession to him, he wasn't an impartial cop, he was a man. A man who hurt. Who was afraid of hurting. "All I know was that I was afraid of losing you. Afraid you'd react just this way—"

Questions materialized. "Who else knows?" she demanded, sinking back into her seat. Embarrassment all but swallowed her up. She couldn't bear having her brothers, her cousins, look at her with pity. "Does everyone know?"

"No, the only people who knew were your mother and me. And Andrew." He saw Janelle's eyes widen and quickly added, "Andrew was the one who told me to put this all behind me and forgive your mother if I still loved her. And I did. With all my heart. I still do."

She would have sworn on a stack of Bibles that there were no secrets in her family. That everything that went on eventually came to light. The laugh was on her, she supposed. Especially if she was the only one who'd been kept in the dark. "And Dax, Troy, Jared, the others, they—"

"They don't know," he told her firmly, before she could finish her question. "Not even Marco knows." This time, his assurance was for her benefit alone. Since the man had called her, Brian wasn't a hundred percent certain that Marco didn't suspect that Janelle was his. "Your mother never told him."

She thought of the phone call, trying to recall if there were any nuances in the man's voice. Had Wayne known? Was there a reason for him to suspect? Or had he known all along?

Was that why he'd sought her out? Or was it just a coincidence, based on nothing more than that she was the daughter of someone he'd once been acquainted with? A man whose wife he'd once had an affair with.

A straw floated by. Desperation made her clutch it as if it could bring her safe passage to shore. Her mother made love with Marco. If she'd had relations during the same period of time with her father— "Maybe there's a mistake, maybe—"

"No mistake, Janelle," he said softly. "The timing," he explained. "Your mother and I hadn't been together as husband and wife for a while when she realized that she was pregnant."

Everything around her crashed and burned. Everything she believed about herself, about her life, her family, none of it was true. It was all based on illusion. On lies.

She had to get out, had to get away. She couldn't think, couldn't breathe. If she stayed here any longer, she was going to pass out. She needed air.

On her feet, Janelle hurried away from the booth. From things that broke her heart. She heard her father calling her name in the background, but all she could focus on was reaching the front door. On putting distance between herself and the pain.

Her hands flat against the door, she pushed it hard so that it groaned as it flew open. Bursting outside, Janelle took in huge gulps of air, filling her lungs as far as she could, then releasing the breath. Trying to pull herself together.

It wasn't helping.

Swallowing an oath, she hurried to her car, knowing only that she had to get out of here.

Sawyer had watched her the entire time. For form's sake, he'd nursed a club soda, much to the bartender's disdain. The latter had walked away muttering something about recovering alcoholics being the death of him. Sawyer had only listened with half an ear as he'd continued to observe Janelle at the booth.

Granted, the lighting left a hell of a lot to be desired, but he had a great ability to focus and concentrate. That more or less helped balance out the deficiencies.

Sawyer settled back, an elbow against the bar he had his back to, prepared to nurse his carbonated drink for about an hour or so, when he saw the look on Janelle's face. Even at this distance, with this light, he could see that she'd just listened to something that had a major impact on her life. A major impact that was unwelcome.

Guessing, he figured it probably had something to do with her extended family. Not his business as long as it didn't involve having a bullet aimed at some part of her body. And she was, after all, with Aurora's chief of detectives, so that pretty much kept her safe.

But whatever thought he'd had about relaxing for the next hour or so instantly fled when he saw Janelle abruptly get up from the table. It seemed completely out of character, especially since she was talking to her father. Rumor had it they enjoyed a healthy, respectful relationship.

Didn't look like that from here. His assignment looked as if she had just been ambushed by an eighteen-foot Gila monster.

Damn it, he thought as he strode quickly through the restaurant toward the door, plowing his way through the crowd, guarding Janelle Cavanaugh just kept getting trickier.

Chapter 9

Janelle's hands were shaking as she took her car keys out of her purse and she dropped them. Her hands never shook, she thought angrily, stooping to pick up the keys. But then, why should she be surprised? It was obvious that she couldn't count on anything being what she thought it was.

Her chest ached.

Aiming the remote at the car, Janelle pressed down on the small button. Nothing happened. She tried again with the same results. Frustration flared so quickly, it almost frightened her. Getting a grip, she stabbed the car key at the keyhole. She managed to scratch the area around it, but miss the opening. Twice.

Finally, Janelle unlocked the door. Swinging it open,

she got in, narrowly avoiding being hit by the door as it swung back. Biting off a curse, she tried to get the key into the ignition. Her hands were shaking harder and she dropped the key ring again.

"Damn it!"

The keys had fallen directly beneath the steering wheel. She had to snake her way under it in order to retrieve them.

By the time she'd secured the keys and sat up, the door on the driver's side was thrown open again.

"Get into the passenger side," Sawyer growled. From where he stood, she looked as if she were having some sort of a breakdown, which meant she was in no condition to drive.

Janelle glared at her intruder. Where the hell had he come from? Her brain felt numb, unable to process anything. It took her a second to remember that she'd left him back at the bar. Why couldn't he have just stayed there?

"Don't tell me what to do," Janelle snapped in response.

Anger he could deal with, but he had a problem coping with the hint of tears on the horizon.

"I'll tell you what to do if I think you need telling," he informed her almost passively, then repeated his instructions. "Now get out and move over to the passenger side." He appraised her face again. Damn it, she was going to cry. He'd bet a month's salary on it. His only chance was to get her too angry to shed tears. "You're in no condition to drive."

What the hell did he care what condition she was in?

She was just his assignment, an inanimate object to guard as far as he was concerned. Only good thing she'd just learned was that she could send him away now.

"You're free," she declared, barely controlling her voice. She waved her hand at him dismissively. "I emancipate you. Go home, Detective Boone. You don't need to guard me anymore."

"Stop babbling and do what I tell you to do."

Her hands gripped the steering wheel. She needed something solid to hold on to, even if just physically. Everything else felt as if it were crumbling around her.

She wasn't a Cavanaugh.

She wasn't anything, she thought.

"Don't you get it?" she demanded angrily. "You don't need to be my guard dog anymore. I'm taking myself off the case. Maybe off the D.A.'s team altogether," she added. She felt completely disoriented. How could she possibly be of any use to anyone else? "Go back to your Batcave and wait for another assignment," she added cryptically.

Rather than stand there and argue with her, Sawyer physically pulled her out of the vehicle. Stunned, Janelle began to shout at him, raining a few choice names down on his head. His face impassive, he didn't seem to hear her.

Hooking his arm around her midsection, Sawyer literally carried her to the other side of the car as if she weighed next to nothing. The fact that she was beating on his chest with fisted hands left no impression whatsoever.

He opened the passenger door and unceremoniously deposited her back into the vehicle. Before Janelle could yelp in protest again, he secured her seat belt around her, brushing against her thighs in the process, then slammed the door. He swiftly rounded the hood and was in the driver's seat before she had a chance to unbuckle her seat belt and make a break for it.

The man was incredibly fast for someone his size, she thought grudgingly.

Sawyer hit the power-lock keypad on his side of the car, locking all four doors at once. Then he pressed down the bypass button, rendering the lock on her side useless. She was locked in.

"This is kidnapping, Boone!" Janelle shouted in frustration.

He checked to see that the key was still in the ignition. It was. With a snap of his wrist, he turned it. Janelle drowned out the sound of the engine coming to life, threatening him.

"You can bring me up on charges later," he replied mildly.

She blew out a long, angry breath. If he was counting on her easygoing nature, he'd miscalculated. "Don't think I won't."

"I'm sure you'll have the full power of your daddy behind you."

Out of the corner of his eye, he saw Janelle stiffen. After backing out of the parking space, he drove toward the exit at the end of the lot. Before turning onto the street, he took the opportunity to glance in her direction. The blood had drained out of her face. "You're pale. What did I say?"

She stared straight ahead, afraid she was going to cry. Damn it, she didn't want to cry in front of this man. He'd probably think it was because of something he'd said.

"Nothing."

The hell it was nothing. He respected boundaries, but not when they crossed over into his territory. And as long as this woman was his responsibility, she was his territory.

He tried again. "Look, I've only been on this assignment a couple of weeks, but it doesn't take long for me to get a handle on some things. You're a talker. If you don't talk, you'll explode."

Guiding the car into the flow of traffic, he waited for her to start.

Instead, she stubbornly dug her heels in. "So?"

"So talk," he ordered impatiently. "Blood's hard to wash out of the upholstery. If anything happens to you, any one of a number of people will be after my head," he reminded her. "Your brothers, your cousins, your father, not to mention the ex-chief of police."

Her family.

Her once and past family, she thought sarcastically.

Damn it, she would have given anything if Marco Wayne and his damn son hadn't come into her life.

Careful, that's your father and brother you're denouncing. Half brother, she amended angrily. Two people who had just robbed her of her happiness and her peace of mind. She hoped they'd both rot in hell.

Janelle continued staring straight ahead, willing her tears back into her ducts. "You've got nothing to worry about from them," she assured Sawyer between clenched teeth.

Sawyer sincerely doubted if he'd ever heard as much hurt packed into a voice as he did right at this minute. She didn't strike him as the hysterical type, or a person given to making dramatic scenes. Yet she seemed to be on the verge of falling apart. Vulnerable and defensive all at the same time.

"Why?" he asked.

"Because you don't," she retorted, crossing her arms before her chest.

Sawyer glanced at her again just as headlights from an oncoming car intruded into the interior of the one he was driving. Illuminating the woman beside him. Her breathing was shallow, her face pale. Again, Janelle seemed on the edge of some sort of anxiety attack.

Sympathy stirred within him. But sympathy wasn't the way to get anything out of her. He instinctively sensed that. "What the hell did your father say to you back there?"

She wouldn't have told him. Of all the people she knew, she would have been more inclined to tell one of the criminals she'd prosecuted than this man. But she felt completely lost, completely directionless and so completely abandoned. She needed to make contact, to grab a lifeline and pull herself out of the mire before she went down for the third time.

Sawyer held out a lifeline.

And suddenly, the words just came tumbling out. Along with the tears she would have rather died than shed. "That he wasn't my father."

OFFICIAL OPINION POLL

ANSWER 3 QUESTIONS AND WE'LL SEND YOU
4 FREE BOOKS AND A FREE GIFT!

0074823 ||||||||||||| ||||||||| ||||||||| FREE GIFT CLAIM # 3953

YOUR OPINION COUNTS!

Please tick TRUE or FALSE below to express your opinion about the following statements:

Q1 Do you believe in "true love"?

"TRUE LOVE HAPPENS ONLY ONCE IN A LIFETIME."
○ TRUE
○ FALSE

Q2 Do you think marriage has any value in today's world?

"YOU CAN BE TOTALLY COMMITTED TO SOMEONE WITHOUT BEING MARRIED."
○ TRUE
○ FALSE

Q3 What kind of books do you enjoy?

"A GREAT NOVEL MUST HAVE A HAPPY ENDING."
○ TRUE
○ FALSE

YES, I have scratched the area below.

Please send me the 4 **FREE BOOKS** and **FREE GIFT** for which I qualify. I understand I am under no obligation to purchase any books, as explained on the back of this card.

I7EI

Mrs/Miss/Ms/Mr _____ Initials _____

BLOCK CAPITALS PLEASE

Surname _____

Address _____

_____

Postcode _____

Visit us online at www.millsandboon.co.uk

THE READER SERVICE™
FREE BOOK OFFER
FREEPOST CN81
CROYDON
CR9 3WZ

NO STAMP
NECESSARY
IF POSTED IN
THE U.K. OR N.I.

Sawyer had had no idea what to expect, but this sure wasn't it. "What?" he demanded.

Janelle had taken a drink, but the glass had been still half-full when she'd suddenly bolted from the restaurant, so she couldn't be drunk. If she wasn't drunk, what the hell was she talking about? Had she had an argument with the chief? Was she one of those females who flew off the handle when she didn't get her way?

He waited for an explanation.

Janelle dragged a hand through her hair, wishing she could somehow erase this day. To pluck out everything that was wrong and make it the way it was before.

Not going to happen. Ever.

She wanted to be alone.

"Look," Janelle began impatiently, "why don't you drive to your place?"

The suggestion caught him completely off guard. Was she propositioning him? Under normal circumstances, if she hadn't been an assignment, if they had just come across one another in that restaurant they'd just vacated, he might have actually been tempted. Something about the woman cut through the barricades he'd thrown up around himself. Something basic that spoke to him.

But she was what she was and right now, he was trying to treat her with kid gloves. Which meant that if this was a proposition, he had to turn her down.

"What?" he asked again.

"That way you can go home and I'll take the car the rest of the way to my place." Each word was an effort.

Sawyer dismissed her suggestion. "My place is not on the way to your place."

"I don't care." Why was he giving her grief? She just wanted to be rid of him. To go home, throw herself on her bed and cry her heart out. Then maybe it wouldn't ache so much. "I'm not trying to save on gasoline right now."

"I'm taking you home." His tone was firm. There was no arguing the point.

Home.

Where was home? Home had always been a state of mind for her, more people than place. Although, if she'd really been pressed to cite where her home was, she would have pointed to the sprawling house where she had grown up. Grown up feeling secure believing she knew who she was and what her place in the universe was.

Idiot, she thought and sighed listlessly. "Yeah, whatever." The next moment, Sawyer was pulling the car over to the side of the road. Now what? She glared at him. "What are you doing?"

He shut off the ignition and turned to look at her. "We're not going any farther until you tell me what's going on."

What did he want from her? Blood?

Now there was an ironic thought, she silently jeered. The blood she'd assumed she had running through her veins, she didn't. All those years she'd kept seeing similarities between herself and her father, her cousins, all of it was just a big joke. There *were* no similarities. Because she wasn't a Cavanaugh.

"I already told you," she insisted, annoyed. "You know as much as I do."

He didn't budge. "I don't think so. You're going to pieces on me and you're not the type to do that."

Her temper snapped. "How the hell do you know what my 'type' is? How do you know anything about me when *I* don't know anything about me."

"Did someone slip you something?" he asked. "I was watching you the whole time, but if a waiter wanted to put something in your drink—"

"Nobody put anything in my drink. My father—" Janelle stopped abruptly the second the word was out of her mouth. He wasn't her father, not anymore. She tried again. "The chief of detectives just pulled the plug on my world, that's all." She spread her hands wide, as if to display something. "This is me when everything goes down the drain."

He still wasn't following her. Crack lawyer or not, she just wasn't making any sense. "You're going to have to start at the beginning."

She was suddenly very tired. Of everything. "Why do I have to start at the beginning?" she demanded hotly.

"Because I can't help you unless I understand what's going on."

"And why would you want to help me?"

"Because I have a merit badge to flesh out," he snapped. "Stop asking stupid questions and just get on with it. Now why are you acting like a chicken with her head cut off?"

Janelle pressed her hand to her chest at the same time that she pressed her lips together. The latter was to keep her voice from cracking. "It's not my head, it's my heart."

"Your heart?" His brow furrowed. "What's the matter with your heart?"

"It's been cut out."

Leaning back, he blew out a breath. For a talkative woman, she rationed out information as if there were a famine underway. "What did you mean when you said that the chief isn't your father?"

She pressed her lips together again. Taking a breath, she let it out slowly before she trusted her voice. "He's not."

How was that possible? Everyone knew the chief of detectives had a daughter and that daughter was currently sitting beside him in the car. "But I thought—"

Janelle laughed, cutting him off. The hollow sound echoed through the interior of the car, mocking her. "That makes two of us."

"You're not getting out of the car until you start making sense," he warned her. "Now what the hell did the chief tell you back there that has you acting like some kind of crazy loon?"

She raised her chin, as if gravity could keep the tears from coming. "He told me that Marco Wayne is my father."

Thunderstruck, Sawyer could only stare at her. "What?"

His expression mirrored what she felt inside, Janelle thought. Except that he was far more in control. She felt as if she were harboring the aftermath of a hurricane inside her chest.

"Exactly." She took a deep breath. What did it matter if this man knew? Everyone would know eventually.

This kind of thing didn't stay hidden forever once the lid was removed. Or blown sky-high.

"Apparently my father—the man I thought was my father," she amended as Sawyer's frown deepened, "my mother and Marco Wayne were all from the same neighborhood. Wayne had a 'thing' for my mother. Seems he kept on having this 'thing' even though he was married and so was she. I'm told that the chief and my mother had their share of problems and Marco took advantage of some downtime in their marriage.

"To put it quite simply, he and my mother had an affair." She spread her hands wide, the smile on her lips taut, painful and utterly without mirth. "And I was the result."

Sawyer took it all in. He'd heard worse. A hell of a lot worse. But this obviously upset her, so he tried to be sympathetic. "And you didn't know?"

"Do I act like I knew?"

"No, you act like somebody just set fire to your whole world."

That was exactly the way she felt. As if everything had just gone up in flames before her very eyes. Janelle laughed softly to herself, although there was no humor in the situation or in the sound of her laughter. As far as she was concerned, there was no humor in anything anymore.

And then her curiosity rallied, getting the better of her. She looked at him, wondering if he was just giving her lip service, or if there was more to it. "You sound as if you know what that's like."

Sawyer watched her for a long moment, then turned back toward the windshield. The taillights of passing cars gleamed like jewels in the night, winking at him, then going dormant.

"Yeah, I know what it's like." *And wish to God I didn't.*

Something in his voice got to her. Still, she didn't think he was above using a ploy.

"How?" she asked. "How could you possibly know what it's like suddenly not to be who you thought you were?"

"I don't," he agreed, his voice flat. "But I do know what it's like to have your whole world incinerate right before your eyes."

This was something he didn't talk about. Not ever. Back in Los Angeles, the men he'd worked with knew what had happened only because of the incident report. Because of the crime stats.

The first officers on the scene had known that the twisted, broken body riddled with bullets they'd discovered in the car was his fiancée, Allison. Until some wild-eyed kid, out for revenge, had picked just that minute to drive by and spray the air with bullets.

Cutting short the life of the sweetest person he had ever known.

"Go on," she urged, daring Sawyer to find a way to equate his pain to hers.

Sawyer heard the challenge in her voice, but it didn't work on him. He wasn't the type that needed a challenge, or felt triumphant when he won, which was often. Winning was just something that he did as a matter of course. And yet he would only get through to her by showing her how she wasn't alone. She wasn't the only one life had kicked square in the face with a cleated combat boot.

"My fiancée was killed in a drive-by shooting."

She stared at him. Hearing the words but not quite absorbing them. "You were engaged?"

"Yeah." For all of three weeks. Happiest three weeks of his life. The only happy three weeks of his life, he amended. "She was a lawyer. Like you," he added, his tone ironic. "Except she represented the other side. Legal aide was her passion, her cause. Like her father." And if it hadn't been for that old man instilling all that in her from the time she could walk, Allison would still be alive today. "She was just in the wrong place at the wrong time."

For the first time, Janelle connected the sadness she'd seen in his eyes to an event. Despite the ache in her chest, she felt her sympathy being aroused. "I'm sorry."

"Yeah." Sawyer said nothing more than that. The subject was closed and he wasn't about to revisit it. After a beat, he turned the key to the right and started up the car again. "You never had a clue about your...the truth?"

Janelle didn't have to review her life; she knew it by heart. There'd never been anything to indicate that she was anyone other than Brian Cavanaugh's daughter. She'd never been treated any differently.

She shook her head. "None."

Sawyer went to the next piece of the puzzle. "When Marco Wayne called you that first day in your office, did he—"

"No. He didn't hint at anything. I was just asking my

father—the chief," she amended. God, this was going to be hard for her. "For advice. I told him that Wayne called, which was when he said he wanted to see me outside the office because he had something to tell me. I never dreamed…" Her voice trailed off. Clearing her throat, she continued. "He said he thought I should take myself off the case because if the defense ever got wind of this…" Again, her voice trailed off and she laughed softly to herself. "I thought he was talking about the phone call."

"But the chief never mentioned anything about you not being his daughter before?" Sawyer pressed. "Never hinted at it?"

"No," she cried. This had come out of the blue, hitting her right between the eyes.

"How did he treat you?"

"What do you mean, how did he treat me?" she asked sharply.

He made a quick left just as the light began to turn red. "When you were growing up under his roof, how did the chief treat you? Did he ignore you, yell at you, make you into his whipping post—"

Janelle took offense for the man she had loved from the first breath she ever took. "No, he did not make me his whipping post."

Sawyer continued his line of questioning as if he didn't hear the annoyance in her voice. "Did you feel he loved you?"

"Yes," she whispered, which made everything that much more painful.

He nodded, taking it all in. "So, what's your problem?" he asked.

"My problem is that he lied to me."

"No," Sawyer corrected, "he didn't tell you. That's different."

"That's what he said." Maybe it was a male thing. "But the truth was buried."

Sawyer approached it from the other side. "Ever think that maybe he didn't like to think about the truth?" This time, rather than pressing down on the accelerator, he came to a stop at the light. "That he loved you despite everything? Takes a big man to do that. To treat you like his own flesh and blood when you weren't. I'd stop feeling sorry for myself if I were you and count my blessings."

He thought of his own childhood. He'd essentially grown up without parents. Without love. "Not all of us have fathers who act as if they give a rat's behind about our welfare. Even if we do happen to share the same DNA code."

She wiped her cheeks with the back of her hand, drying the tears. Though she was angry at Sawyer's intrusive questions, she was even more angry that she had fallen apart in front of him. And angriest of all because, underneath the hurt, she knew he was right. It still hurt with the searing pain of a new wound, and only time would make that go away. And only time would help her come to terms with who she was in the scheme of things.

Would Brian Cavanaugh even want her around now that she knew? Now that the secret was finally out?

She glanced at the rocklike profile of the man to her left. He was abrupt, brash and direct. And for some reason, she couldn't fault him for it. But that didn't mean she had to like the way he went about things. "Anyone ever tell you that you belong in the diplomatic corps?"

"There's been talk," he told her with a completely straight face as he turned her car into her apartment complex.

It started to rain.

Chapter 10

By the time they reached her door, they were close to drenched. The sky had just opened up and poured.

As she raced for her door and shelter, Janelle couldn't help thinking that this rain was a metaphor for her life. The forecast had made no mention of rain and the sky had been clear all day.

The downpour had come out of nowhere. Just like her father's revelation.

Her father. What did she call him now? Brian? Chief? He wasn't really her dad anymore. And yet, in the truest sense of the word, in the truest spirit, he really was.

Damn, she had never been this confused in her entire life.

After getting the door open, she walked in and immediately flipped on the light switch. Without
thinking, she shook her head, sending raindrops flying
from her hair.

"I'll get a towel," she volunteered as she hurried over
to the small linen closet just outside her bedroom door.

Sawyer shucked his jacket and threw it over the back
of the closest kitchen chair. His jeans adhered to him
like a second skin. "Make it a big one."

It took her a second to realize what he was saying.
Of course, she hadn't meant they'd be making use of the
same towel at the same time.

"I'll get two towels," she corrected. Once she pulled
them out, she crossed back to him and handed Sawyer a
large, light blue bath towel. "You should have gone to your
car," she told him as she rubbed the towel against her hair.

Sawyer did what he could with the towel, but it was
clear they were both going to have to change their
clothes. He looked over toward her, trying not to notice
that her blouse became transparent when wet.

"Don't like me dripping on your rug?"

"It's not that." She rubbed the towel against her
face, then retired it. "But you could be on your way
home by now."

He had a change of clothes here, and there was no
reason for him to leave tonight. He supposed that she
was too upset to see the situation logically. "Nothing at
home that won't keep."

Finished for now, Sawyer draped the towel around
his neck, wrapping his fingers around the ends. It

amazed him how wet they'd gotten in just a short hundred yards. Especially her. Janelle's clothing was sticking to her torso in ways that fired a man's imagination. He would have been less than human not to notice. And superhuman if it didn't affect him.

He allowed himself a moment, then raised his eyes to hers. "I'd better change into something dry. You, too," he advised.

She shrugged. Right now, it was all she could do to concentrate on breathing. Anything else seemed like too much of an effort. It took several seconds for her brain to catch up and process what he'd just said. Sawyer was going to change clothes. But he'd only get them wet again when he went to his car.

The light dawned. "Aren't you going home?"

He looked at her patiently, an adult allowing a child to prattle on. "No."

There was no reason for him to stay any longer, although she had to admit that the prospect of being alone with her thoughts was not nearly as desirable as it had been half an hour ago.

"But I don't need a bodyguard anymore," she reminded him. "I'm going to ask the D.A. to take me off the case." With any luck, citing "personal" reasons would be enough for Kleinmann. She was not about to tell him the real reason.

Damn, but he wished she'd go and change already. Or stand where the light didn't bathe over her body that way. "Wayne's men don't know that," Sawyer replied mildly. "Nothing's changed."

"Except for everything," she whispered. Her knees felt like soggy cotton and she sank down on the sofa.

Sawyer watched as a damp imprint formed on the cushion around the perimeter of her thighs. He doubted she was even aware of it. But he was. Damn, but he was.

He forced his thoughts elsewhere. "If the chief hadn't told you about it, nothing would have changed," he told her.

"But he did tell me."

"That's the only thing that's changed," Sawyer pointed out. "Your knowledge of the situation. The chief isn't going to suddenly treat you differently, your brothers aren't. Nobody's going to step out of the equation if you don't take yourself out of it first."

She supposed it made sense. She wanted to believe what he was saying to her. But she just felt so shell-shocked, it was hard to hang on to any sort of stabilizing thought.

Janelle looked at him, wondering why he was being so nice to her. He'd always acted as if he couldn't wait for this assignment to be over; now he was comforting her. "Why do you care?"

"I don't," he replied simply. "I just don't like illogical behavior." And he liked the lost look in her eyes even less. He supposed he might still react to the human condition. There was no other reason why he was trying to get her to come around. "Now get up off the sofa and get out of those wet clothes."

He watched the smallest hint of a smile bloom on her lips. "Are you coming on to me, Detective?"

Sawyer shoved his hands into his back pockets. They were wet and made the relatively innocuous movement more difficult.

"When I do, Cavanaugh, you won't have to ask," was all he said.

When. Not *if, when.*

Janelle had no idea why, in the midst of all the turmoil swirling around her, that single word somehow made her feel better. She was punchy and tired. And hollow beyond belief.

With a nod, Janelle rose to her feet. She noticed he made no effort to back away, no effort to either give her her space, or take it over. He remained where he was. Watching her walk out.

She paused and turned around just before she opened her bedroom door. "Detective."

He raised an eyebrow. "Yeah?"

Was it her imagination or was his voice softer somehow? Gentler. Right now, she doubted every single thing she'd thought she once knew. She needed an anchor and there wasn't one. But he'd been kind when it wasn't in his nature, and she appreciated this.

"Thank you." She closed the door to her room before he could respond.

Stephen Woods looked at her incredulously. She would have rather gone to Kleinmann with this, but there'd been a sudden personal emergency. Something about the D.A.'s mother taking a turn for the worse. Janelle knew that the woman had been ill for some time. Kleinmann and his wife had left for New York on a predawn flight, forcing Janelle to seek out Woods instead.

"You want to be taken off of the Wayne case?" Woods asked.

Want was the wrong word, she thought. *Need* was more like it. "Yes." She nodded.

Woods leaned over his desk, alert and concerned. He was a nice man beneath the pompous veneer, she thought. "Did something happen, Janelle? We can double the number of people guarding—"

"No, nothing happened." At least not in the sense that Woods meant it. No one had shot at her. She would have actually preferred that to learning what she'd learned.

And then a knowing look came over his thin, sharp features. "It's that detective, isn't it? Boone. Really raw and rough around the edges." He nodded his perfectly coiffured head. "He'd be hard for anyone to deal with. We could request someone else for you."

"It's not him," she said. Damn, she hated asking for a favor, no matter what the reason behind it was. "This is personal." Woods looked at her. She could almost see his mind working, trying to puzzle things out. She decided to go with a lesser truth. Who would have known the very thing that had caused her world to blow up would turn out to be her saving grace? "Marco Wayne called me."

Woods's jaw dropped as if it had suddenly become unhinged. "He what?"

"Marco Wayne called me. Here at the office." She knew numbers would be checked. They needed to be above reproach on this, above any appearances of wrongdoing or impropriety. "Said that his son was innocent, that he wanted a fair trial for the kid." She pretended to shrug carelessly. "You know, the usual things a father would say."

Woods snorted. "Except that he's a major crime figure."

"He's still a father," Janelle insisted. Wayne had sounded sincere when he'd spoken to her. Maybe it was all part of an act, but having been raised in an atmosphere where family came first, she could understand even an organized-crime lieutenant feeling concerned. "Anyway," she continued, "even though nothing improper was said, the very fact that he did call me might be something the defense will want to use against the case we have. So, I thought that in the interest of making sure that this isn't thrown out of court on some shaky, fabricated technicality, I'd take myself off the case."

Woods leaned back in his chair and blew out a breath, his small brown eyes never leaving her face. "I don't know what to say, Janelle. This is the biggest case of your career."

It was, she thought. Until everything had been turned upside down. "I know."

He shook his head in wonder. "I must say, you Cavanaughs are an altruistic bunch."

You Cavanaughs. The words echoed in her head, mocking her.

"Yes," she finally replied, "we are."

Except that she wasn't part of the "we" anymore, no matter what kind of arguments Detective Boone raised to the contrary.

The ache in her chest grew larger.

Sawyer wasn't in her office when she returned from her meeting with Woods. Gone, she thought. Like a thief in the night. She would have expected Sawyer to have at least offered a civil goodbye. But, she supposed he didn't want to waste any time putting distance between them.

Either that, or he'd gotten a call from his superior, re-assigning him.

Janelle crossed over to the chair that he'd occupied for the last few weeks and stared at it. After seeing him there for so long, it seemed odd to have him gone. If she took in a deep breath, she could still smell the barest hint of his cologne. His scent.

She blew out a breath. *Get a grip, Nelle.*

He'd left his jacket, she realized.

It took her only a second of debating, if that long, before she jettisoned her honorable inclination and began going through the pockets. If she was lucky, the book he'd been reading all this time would still be there.

"Looking for something?"

She was surprised she didn't yelp. As it was, he'd startled her and she dropped the jacket as she swung around. She could feel color and heat creeping up her cheeks.

"I thought you'd left." The statement came out sur-prisingly devoid of any stammering, especially consid-ering that her insides felt as if they'd been dumped into a blender and left on high.

"I did." Crossing to her, Sawyer picked up the jacket.

She didn't see any amusement in his eyes. No condemnation, either. "To the bathroom," he elaborated. "Even superheroes have to go once in a while."

She had no idea why she was happy that he hadn't just vanished out of her life without a whisper. It shouldn't have mattered to her one way or another. If anything, she should have felt relieved when she'd thought he was gone, not had this oddly sad sensation echoing through her.

Janelle pushed forward to the inevitable parting. Like tearing off a Band-Aid, she needed to do this quickly. "I told Woods and he's taking me off the case."

Still holding his jacket, he studied her for a second, then nodded. "You told him that Wayne called you."

That shouldn't have been his first guess and she didn't like the fact that Sawyer seemed so confident that he could read her so easily. Especially since he could.

"How did you know?" she asked.

"Logic." He looked down at the jacket she'd been rifling through when he'd walked in. "I didn't take you for a pickpocket."

She hated getting caught. This was not one of her better days. "I just wanted to see what you were reading."

He patted the pocket, but left the book inside. "Curiosity killed the cat."

She always thought of that as a stupid saying. "I'm bigger than a cat—and more resourceful," she added. Then waited.

After a beat, a slow, lazy smile moved over his lips, curving it. Reaching into the right pocket, he took out a book that was close to shapeless from countless readings. He held it up to her.

"Henry V?" Janelle read, then raised her eyes to his. "Shakespeare? You're reading Shakespeare?" Sawyer did *not* look like the Shakespeare type.

"Man's got interesting things to say," Sawyer replied, answering the quizzical expression on her face. Slipping the jacket on, he shoved the book back into his pocket. "Stay safe, Cavanaugh," he said as he made his way to the door.

She nodded. "You, too."

He was leaving, she thought, just the way she'd wanted him to since the first moment he'd walked into her life.

The office felt empty the minute he was on the other side of the door.

In place of the Wayne case, Janelle was quickly assigned two new cases. She spent the remainder of the day acquainting herself with the particulars of both. Lunch came in; she did not go out.

The first case was a hit-and-run involving a homeless man and a female advertising executive on her way up. The woman had clearly panicked and fled the scene of the crime. Her bad fortune was that there had been an eye witness at the taco stand across the street. The other case had to do with a difference of opinion over a baseball game at a trendy sports bar. The argument had gotten out of hand and one patron had beaten the other within an inch of his life. Plenty of witnesses, lots of different viewpoints.

Her head began to ache just after one o'clock. By the end of the day, when added to her already significant caseload, the two new cases left her feeling overwhelmed. And strangely empty.

When Janelle finally made her way out of the building to the rear parking lot, it was almost eight. Only a few cars pockmarked the lot. She guessed that even the parking structure was close to empty. Most of the people who worked in the building preferred the structure. It was cooler in the summer, warmer in the winter and it protected vehicles from the elements, more importantly, from the sun. But she liked being out in the open.

Too many spooky movies as a kid, she supposed, mocking herself.

She noticed the black stretch limousine at the same time that the sound of her footsteps mingling with someone else's registered. It took her a second to remember that she no longer had a shadow. Sawyer wasn't there to haunt her every move.

The second she turned around, a big, burly man with a lived-in face and in a rumpled dark suit took hold of her arm. He smelled faintly of onions when he spoke.

"Mr. Wayne would like a word with you."

Startled, she looked at him. He had enough lines on his face to qualify him as an honorary shar-pei. Another man seemed to materialize out of the darkness, taking her other arm. Between them, she was hustled over to a waiting black limousine.

"We're not that far from the police department," she

warned them, adding, "I'm not on the case anymore." She might as well have been reciting the Korean alphabet. Her words seemed to bounce off the two men. Neither even indicated that they heard her.

The door to the limousine opened and she was deposited roughly inside. The next second, the door closed and she found herself sealed in with the other occupant in the rear of the vehicle.

The air-conditioning was on in the car. The man sitting at the opposite end of the richly upholstered seat had on a camel-colored topcoat. It was unbuttoned and the suit beneath would have probably paid the salaries of five uniformed policemen for a month.

She'd heard that Marco Wayne liked nothing but the best. Tolerated nothing less. He had a full head of silver hair and the look of a man who had long since stopped trusting anyone.

Still, time had been kind to him. He didn't look his age. She'd done her research on him last night, finding out all she could. Knowledge was thought to be power. Janelle didn't feel like someone in power, but she did her best not to show it.

Janelle met his gaze dead-on, knowing that to look away would be an indication of fear. Marco Wayne did not respect people who feared.

"I'm not on the case anymore, Mr. Wayne."

His head inclined ever so slightly. His voice was rich when he spoke. "I know."

How had it become public knowledge so fast? Or did he have someone on the inside? The news media hadn't approached her for a comment. They would have if the story had been broken. So that meant that Wayne had someone reporting to him from inside the D.A.'s office. Which in turn meant they were all vulnerable.

She'd think about that later. Right now, she needed to get out of this limousine in one piece. She took solace in the fact that the car wasn't moving. "Then you know there's nothing I can do."

"Now that, I don't know," Wayne contradicted. There was a smile on his face, but it didn't reach his eyes. "I'm told that you are very resourceful. That you don't just go with the flow, take someone else's word for things. You examine, dissect."

"Meaning?"

He leaned forward just an inch. "Meaning that Tony was framed. Someone else's words put him behind bars."

She wasn't going to bring out the violins just yet. "That and the kilo of coke found in his possession," she reminded him.

Wayne's dark eyes narrowed into slits. "That was planted."

"Why?" Janelle asked. "By who?" If he wanted her to believe him, then he was going to have to come up with something better than just his word. She needed evidence to the contrary, motive, something to work with.

Wayne nodded, as if he expected nothing less from someone with his blood. This time, the smile she saw take hold looked genuine. As if she'd passed some unknown test and he approved of her.

"Tony's a good boy," he told her. "I've kept him as far away from my business as possible." *Business,* she thought, what an odd term for extortion and trafficking in flesh peddling and drugs. "I'm sure you know that I'm number two in the organization."

Was he trying to impress her? Scare her? Flatter her? "I've done my homework on you," she responded.

"Backbiting and the elimination of competition doesn't just happen in the corporate world," Wayne informed her.

She tried to make sense of what he was telling her. "Are you saying someone has it in for you, so they're trying to destroy your son?"

"I wouldn't stay down." She saw anger color his face even though he never raised his voice. "Tony is being used to keep me in line."

She wondered what would happen if she suddenly opened the door and ran. The man who had "escorted" her into the limo was undoubtedly standing right outside her door. "Do you have anyone in particular in mind?"

The answer came without hesitation. "Charlie Wentworth. He wants to be number one when the old man passes."

That would be Salvatore Perelli, she thought. "And the 'old man' favors you."

Again Marco inclined his head. "We're from the same neighborhood."

"Then he should help you settle it." She raised her chin, refusing to be intimidated. "In any event, I'm out of it. I can't help you, Mr. Wayne."

Wayne's voice was low, confident. "You're far from out of it, Janelle." His smile was one of reminiscence. "You remind me a lot of your mother."

Was that just an innocent comment? Or his way of intimating something more? Her stomach tightened as she deliberately baited him. "They say my stubbornness comes from my father."

The short laugh was just a little cruel. "Brian Cavanaugh is a good man. I always liked him, even after he took your mother away from me." He paused a moment, as if debating something, then continued. "I knew she'd have a better life with him, even though materially, I could give her more." He paused again, studying her. She could almost feel his eyes passing over her. "Brian told you, didn't he?"

To play dumb seemed pointless. "He told me."

Wayne nodded. "He doesn't know that I know. Keeping quiet was my gift to Susan. No one else knows."

But they would, if it served his purpose, she thought. "For now."

"Ever," he assured her. "That's not a weapon in my arsenal." The statement was firm. A promise. "But Anthony *is* your half brother. And he's being framed." His eyes held her prisoner. "Help him." It was half a plea, half an order.

Before she could protest, or say anything further, Wayne rapped once on his window. The next moment, the door on her side opened and the same man who'd ushered her in was helping her out of the limousine. Gently this time. She stared at him.

Without saying a word, he got into the vehicle in her place.

Janelle watched as the door closed again. A moment later, the black limousine sped away, leaving her standing alone in the parking lot.

Chapter 11

"What the hell did you think you were doing?"

A scream throbbed within Janelle's throat but she managed to bite it back. Her heart pounding, she swung around even as she pressed her hand to her chest, physically reassuring herself the organ hadn't just jumped out of her body.

Sawyer was almost right on top of her, and she hadn't even heard him approach. "Don't you make any noise?" she demanded.

"I left my brass band in my other pants. What the hell were you doing, getting into that limousine with those thugs?"

He'd come out of the building just in time to see her emerging from the stretch limo. Between the street lamps and the moon, there'd been enough light for him to make out the two men who had been standing guard on either side of the black vehicle. He'd recognized both as being Wayne's henchmen. Sawyer had been about to call for backup when he'd seen the taller of the two men opening the rear door. The next second, Janelle had been helped out of the vehicle.

"I didn't exactly have much choice," she retorted. "One minute, I was leaving the building, the next, these two goons are making like silent bookends, blocking my way. The one that looked like a rumpled pile of clothing said that Marco wanted to see me."

"And?" Sawyer pressed.

Janelle gestured dismissively. She was still somewhat shaken, but she didn't like Sawyer's tone. "And he saw me."

"And?" he demanded again. When she looked up at him almost defiantly, he struggled to hold on to his temper. He didn't need this. You'd think the woman being part of the D.A.'s office, knowing the kind of man Wayne was, would play by the rules no matter *what* her relationship to the man. "Look, Cavanaugh, this is no time to suddenly start limiting your vocabulary. In case it escaped you, Marco Wayne doesn't exactly spend all his time playing chess with the pope and working on his needlepoint."

Her eyes narrowed. If he'd acted concerned, she could have put up with his questions, but he was behaving as if this was all one hell of an inconvenience for him. She was just inches away from turning on her heel and walking away from him. "Your point, Boone?"

"The man's dangerous," he told her between clenched teeth.

Okay, maybe he was concerned and he just had lousy communication skills. She'd give him the benefit of the doubt.

"He didn't threaten me," she told him, some of the anger leeching out of her voice. "And he knows that I'm his daughter." Mild surprise creased Sawyer's brow. "He more or less indicated that he never tried to make any contact because he knew my mother wanted to try to work things out with my father. It was his 'gift' to her, to pretend that he didn't know about me."

Sawyer could think of a dozen different reasons, all a great deal more selfish, why the man had never got in contact with his daughter before. "But he's reaching out to you now."

She was beginning to read Sawyer like a book. He didn't trust Wayne. Not that she blamed him. She wouldn't have either. Except that she had seen the crime lieutenant's face just now, seen his eyes when he'd spoken of his son. "Because he's afraid for his son. He also has a theory."

Sawyer laughed shortly. "I just bet he does."

She began to walk toward her car. Sawyer had no choice but to fall into place. "Wayne thinks that one of the other lieutenants in the organization is trying to gain control over him. This ploy with Tony is to show him what can happen if he steps out of line."

Sawyer stopped walking and put his hand on her shoulder to stop her in her tracks. "And if Marco decides to cooperate with this other lieutenant, the 'evidence' will suddenly disappear?"

"Could be," she allowed and then she shrugged. "Your guess is as good as mine—except that I don't really believe that Wayne will actually give in to anyone. His life won't be worth a counterfeit nickel if he allows anyone around him to think that he's weak."

Sawyer regarded her for a moment, thinking. Playing out scenarios in his head. "So you're supposed to be his only hope."

She tried to gauge what Sawyer was thinking. "You make it sound as if that's impossible."

"I didn't say that." They resumed walking. Her vehicle was only a few feet away. "But if you're going to blow holes in your own case, and soon—" they both knew that the beginning of the trial was only a couple of weeks away "—you're going to need help."

"It's not my case anymore."

"Right. Then I guess you can blow holes in it all you want," he said sarcastically. "It'll only mean your career in the D.A.'s office. Someone aims to get brownie points with this conviction," he reminded her. To lose the high-profile case before a public that was addicted to continuous media coverage would be an embarrassment to both Woods and the D.A. Neither was likely to forget who was responsible if that occurred.

Stopping by her car, Janelle ignored the obvious. "You said something about help." Her eyes held his. "Are you volunteering?" When he made no effort to deny it or set her straight, she had her answer, or at least part of it. "Why?"

He shrugged. "I'd feel guilty, leaving you dog-paddling for your life in the middle of a stormy ocean."

The image was far from flattering, but she let it go. "Kleinmann's a stickler for honesty, but he's out of town. Woods is a good man, but he has his eye on the prize—which is getting Kleinmann's seat one day." She said what they were both thinking. "If he convicts the mob lieutenant's son—"

Sawyer nodded. "He might be a shoo-in. Yeah, I know."

She wouldn't have thought of Sawyer as being altruistic. Or an ally. It left her doubting her own powers of evaluation. It also left her with a warm feeling. "So you're throwing in your lot with me."

He shrugged as if it was of no consequence. "Looks like."

"And when do you plan to do this?" It wasn't like him to be illogical. She'd learned that much about him. "Now that you don't have to be my bodyguard, they'll reassign you." A thought occurred to her. "Maybe even to guard whoever Woods decides to replace me with."

Guarding someone else would have him on the premises, but would definitely get in the way of what he wanted to do. Which was a little investigating on his own. There were strings to pull and a few favors to call in. He told himself it was in the interest of justice, but if he were being really honest with himself, he'd have to admit that it also had something to do with eyes the color of clover in the spring.

"I have a month and a half of vacation time coming to me," he told her casually.

"A month and a half?" she echoed incredulously. She was lucky if she could scrounge up four extra days at Christmas.

He nodded. "That's after I lose the five I carried over from two years ago."

She did a quick tally in her head. That meant that Sawyer hadn't used *any* of his time. "Don't you take vacations?"

Taking vacations, packing to go to some strange place he'd never been to before just to say he'd done it, had never appealed to him. "To do what?"

"Something you enjoy."

There was a half shrug involving one shoulder that carelessly rose and fell. "I enjoy being a cop."

And right now, she was glad of it. But that only went so far in a person's life. She began to think of him in more human terms. "But there's more to life than that."

He'd had more. And it had been taken away from him. He didn't need to go through that again. "Not that I've noticed." He didn't want anything that remotely passed for pity. "Look, do you want my help or not?"

"I want it, I want it," she assured him with feeling. "I just feel a little guilty taking away your time, that's all."

"Don't." It was more of a command than a suggestion or request. "I don't do what I don't want to do," he told her.

"Except act as a 'babysitter,'" she recalled the sentiment he'd expressed the first day on the job.

Sawyer made no comment, except for the flicker of annoyance in his eyes. He nodded toward her vehicle. "Now stay there until I get my car and come back around to your side of the lot."

"Yes, sir." She saluted. And saw a hint of a smile flirt with his lips as he turned away to head back to get his own vehicle.

Janelle got into her car and waited. Funny how things worked themselves out. When he had first been assigned to her, she would have never thought she'd be in this position. She needed him. Needed him because she felt that this—digging into the evidence against Tony Wayne one more time to make sure that it was all above board—was something she had to do and no way was she going to ask anyone in the family—or what had been her family up to a day ago—to put their careers, much less themselves, on the line for her in order to see this through.

Sawyer, on the other hand, was volunteering. Insisting was more like it. He seemed to thrive on the idea that a wrong move would put him in seven kinds of jeopardy. And she did need someone to help her because no way could she do her own work and this on the sly. Asking for a short leave of absence would get her nowhere since they were short-handed right now. Last month two of their assistants had quit to go into private practice, where the hours might have been just as long, but the financial rewards were far greater and, for many, that was the bottom line. Mortgages were rarely paid by an esthetic feeling of having done the right thing.

Janelle cracked a window. It was getting warm in the car. Finally, she saw Sawyer's dark blue vehicle emerge out of the parking structure. He leaned out and gestured for her to leave the lot first. She couldn't shake the image of a sheep being herded to another pasture. Maybe that was his intent.

Damn, but she wished she could turn to someone else. But in reality, she couldn't. This was something she felt she had to do. She couldn't even put a well-defined reason to it, other than the fact that she didn't want to be responsible for convicting someone on falsified evidence. That he was supposedly her half brother had nothing to do with it.

Half brother. The term mocked her. She wanted the three whole ones she'd known and loved since birth. She wanted her old life, her old confidence back, she thought as she drove into the night.

True to his word, Sawyer followed her all the way home. The guest parking spaces were all filled and she saw him pass her carport as he went in search of somewhere to leave his vehicle. She knew he'd want her to wait for him, but she didn't have the patience to sit in her car any longer. A restlessness ate at her.

Janelle pulled her car into her space and got out. Holding on to her keys, she hurried to unlock her door. As she was about to step over the threshold, she looked down and saw that someone had slipped a note under her door.

In this day and age of e-mail, text messaging and answering machines, a note under the door seemed old-fashioned.

The moment the thought occurred to her, she knew who the note was from.

Stooping down, she picked it up, turned on the light and opened the note. Janelle smiled to herself. She was right.

> Nelle,
> I'm giving you your space for now. I know finding out about Marco Wayne at this point in your life was a huge shock. I realize now that I made a mistake keeping this from you. But you have to know that I did it only because I didn't want to lose you. You are, and always have been, very precious to me. You are my daughter in every meaningful sense of the word and always will be. Whether or not you want to have anything to do with me right now, I'll still be here, waiting, to talk to you whenever you feel like talking.
> Love, Dad.

Janelle sighed as she stood there in the doorway, holding the note against her chest. She felt torn, confused. Wanting nothing more than never to have found out, never to have her world rocked this way.

And yet, ignorance had never been the path she'd chosen.

Janelle blew out a breath, shaking her head.

The next moment, she found herself being roughly pushed into her apartment. The door slammed loudly behind her. Sawyer flipped the lock, then turned to glare accusingly down at her.

"What the hell is wrong with you?"

Her temper snapped. "You know, I'm getting a little tired of your attitude," she stormed, refusing to be cowed. "Maybe this was a bad idea. Maybe you'd better just go home."

"You were standing there, the door opened, the light on, an open invitation to any maniac who thinks there's a contract out on you. The only thing you were missing was a big red arrow suspended from the roof, pointing at you." Janelle began to protest, but he cut her off. As far as he was concerned, there was nothing she could say in her defense. "Just because you took yourself off the case, Cavanaugh, doesn't mean you're out of the woods. No pun intended," he tagged on. "If Wayne's right and this is being done to control him, maybe whoever's doing it knows that he's gone to you asking for help in clearing his son. If you're eliminated, there will be no help coming from your quarter."

He made it hard to argue with him, even though she wanted to. Temporarily surrendering, she said, "Maybe I should call in the others."

"Others?"

"My family."

Despite his annoyance, he couldn't help noticing that the term had rolled off her tongue. She still thought of them as her family—and should.

She was coming round, he thought. The hurt, the wild, disoriented look was all but gone from her eyes.

He wondered if it was because of what he'd said to her earlier, or if the note she was holding had anything to do with her change of heart.

In either case, she'd forgotten something. "You don't want to risk any of them," he reminded her. That had been her reasoning for accepting his offer to help.

"And you're expendable?"

"I am to you."

That was exactly what she *didn't* want him to think. She wasn't like that. She didn't use people. Even people who made her reach her flashpoint faster than she thought possible.

"That's not true," she protested.

Sawyer smiled. He had a nice smile, she realized.

"Okay," he amended, "I'm less irreplaceable."

There was a knock on the door. Instantly, Sawyer reverted back to the man she'd grown accustomed to seeing. Hard-edged, dangerous, every nerve ending alert.

"You expecting anyone?" he asked her. Janelle shook her head.

Sawyer motioned her back. The next second, he was drawing his weapon and taking the safety off. Holding the gun in both hands, he inclined his head ever so slightly, silently giving her a cue even as he motioned for her to step back even farther.

Janelle took a deep breath. "Who is it?"

"Open the door, Janelle," a low, powerful voice instructed. "It's Uncle Andrew."

Janelle sighed with relief and moved forward. She was about to unlock the door, but Sawyer held up his hand and blocked her path. He looked through the peephole to assure himself that Janelle's visitor was indeed the ex-chief of police.

It was. Sawyer stepped back.

"I know his voice," Janelle informed him. Sawyer felt he was doing what was necessary, but she hated being treated like a helpless child. She flipped the lock and pulled open the door.

Why did seeing her uncle suddenly flood her with a myriad of emotions? She caught herself fighting back tears as she struggled to keep from just throwing herself into his arms.

Andrew gave the tall, silent young man with the un-holstered weapon the once-over as he walked into the apartment. He usually considered it his business to know every aspect of his family's lives and be up on what was happening on the police force he had once headed.

In the prime of his life, having lived through more than most men could cite, Andrew Cavanaugh was regarded as a loving, benevolent patriarch by the entire Cavanaugh clan. The position had passed on to him ever since his own father had died many years ago. The oldest of three brothers, all of whom had entered into law enforcement, Andrew had assumed the mantle graciously and naturally. To Andrew, nothing was as important as family. Not even the law, which his wife had once called his all-consuming mistress.

During times of trouble, large or small, Andrew could always be counted on. He'd been both uncle and father to Patrick and Patience when their own father, his brother Mike, had been less than noble in his behavior and in his treatment of his family.

Born between Andrew and Brian, Michael could never shake the feeling that he was not as good as either one of his brothers. He'd coped with his feelings of inadequacy in a time-dishonored manner. By drinking his pain away. It was Andrew who tried to make him come around and Andrew who was there for Patrick and Patience, as well as for Mike's wife, when things became too rocky.

He was wearing the same grim expression now as he'd had the night Mike had been killed in the line of duty.

For a second, Janelle could feel her heart freeze in her chest. Was it about one of the others? Had one of her brothers, her cousins or her father been shot? She was afraid even to phrase the question. "Uncle Andrew, what's wrong?"

Before answering, his dark blue eyes shifted toward Sawyer. "Give us a minute, will you?" It was a polite request, but not one he expected to be contested.

Sawyer inclined his head. "I'll be in the back bedroom if you need me," he told Janelle.

The second Sawyer was gone, Andrew looked at his niece. When he spoke, his voice was as stern as she'd ever heard him.

"Now you listen to me, missy, I don't know what's going through that head of yours, but just because you found out something that doesn't sit right with you doesn't change who you are." His steely eyes held her prisoner, not allowing her to dispute a word. "You are

Janelle Cavanaugh. You were given that name and a place in our hearts the day you were born. And nothing that's said or 'discovered,'" he added with a touch of sarcasm, "changes any of that."

Andrew paused for a moment, fighting with his own emotions, then slipped his arm around her shoulders. "I saw Brian's face the day you were born—you can't fake love like that. We've been twenty-eight years raising you," he informed her. "We're not about to allow a parting of the ways now because of some 'accident of birth.' Do I make myself clear?"

There was concern in his face. Concern, she knew, over her feelings. She remembered the last time he'd looked so concerned. It was when his wife, Rose, had disappeared. When Aunt Rose's car had been found in the lake the next day, everyone had thought she was dead. For fifteen years, they'd thought that. Everyone but Andrew.

And everyone but Andrew had been wrong.

Her uncle was a man of strength, of faith and of convictions. And from the sound of it, he wasn't about to release her from her family ties.

Which was just fine with her.

"Perfectly," she replied.

"Good," he pronounced and then hugged her. Hard. "So I can tell Brian the problem is over?"

She took in a deep breath and then let it out. And then nodded.

"Good," he repeated. "Because the next step was going to be kidnapping you. Sticky business, kidnapping." And then he smiled, running a hand over her hair just as he'd done when she was a little girl. "We've missed you at the table."

And she missed them. But life kept insisting on getting in the way. "I've been very busy lately."

The look he gave her told her that was no excuse. "So have the others."

She thought of the crowded, noisy breakfasts, the celebrations they'd all shared together. She suddenly realized how lucky she was that her father hadn't turned her mother out when she'd confessed her infidelity. That he had taken her mother back and, in doing so, had allowed her to grow up secure and happy.

"I'll try to make it," she promised.

His work done, Andrew began to leave. But he paused at the door. "Do more than try, Nelle. By the way, bring the bodyguard," he said, nodding toward the back. "He looks like he could use a good meal."

She had no idea why that made her smile, but it did. "Yes, Uncle Andrew."

His eyes crinkled as he laughed. "That's my girl."

It had a nice ring to it, Janelle thought as she locked the door behind her uncle.

Chapter 12

The moment the front door closed, Sawyer came up behind her. If she hadn't turned just then, she wouldn't have known he was there. The man moved like smoke, which made her wonder where he had picked up that talent and why.

"I can see where you get your pushiness from," he said.

He'd been listening, and she didn't take that kindly. Nor did she appreciate his comment, seeing as how she wasn't really related to the man who had just left, no matter how much she wanted to be. It made for a very sore spot.

Janelle's eyes narrowed as she gave him a look. He could almost read what was going through her head.

"Genes aren't everything," he told her in a mild voice

that was backed by experience. "Association had a lot to do with forming who and what you are."

She wanted to argue with him because he just set her off. But in her heart, she wanted him to be right. Because she *was* like the Cavanaughs, not like the mob leader who had begat her with no more thought than a fruit fly had to its progeny. She'd spent the last eighteen hours reading up on Wayne. The man was nothing like her—except for the exhibition of his love for his son. And who knew, that could still be an act for a reason she had no clue to. Yet.

Janelle paused for a second, silently wondering what it was about the man in front of her that made her want to argue so much. Made her want to resist whatever he said even though she actually agreed with him. It wasn't like her to be unreasonable. She always had a reason for her actions, even if they only made sense to her. This didn't.

The question shimmered before her, waiting for an answer. She had none. For now, she supposed, it would be better just to bury the question.

"Yeah, maybe," she allowed with a casual shrug of her shoulders. And then she smiled, remembering Andrew's parting words. "Uncle Andrew wants me to bring you to breakfast tomorrow. Or some morning," she expanded, leaving herself some wiggle room if she was running late tomorrow.

"Breakfast?"

"You know, morning meal. Cereal, pancakes, eggs. The one nutritionists all say is so important for you."

"I know what breakfast is," he retorted. He moved

into the kitchen and opened the refrigerator. The man was acting as if this were his home, she thought, annoyed. "Why's he inviting me?" Sawyer took out the coffee can and put it on the counter. Opening the cupboard directly above the coffeemaker, he took out a fresh filter.

With a sigh, she took the filter from him and placed it in the coffeemaker, then measured out heaping spoonfuls of coffee grounds and poured them into the filter. "He makes breakfast for the family every morning. He likes having family come by and he likes cooking."

Sawyer poured cold water into the mug he'd left on the sink this morning and dumped the contents into the urn. The machine began to gurgle immediately. "I'm not family."

She frowned at the mug he'd retired to the counter. The inside looked permanently stained. Her health instincts getting the better of her, she took out a scrub pad and applied it to the dark brown coating on the interior of the mug. "Technically, neither am I—"

"Don't start," he warned, raising a brow. He didn't want her to cry because he had no idea what to do when confronted with her tears. Other than walk away. But he couldn't walk away from Janelle. For a number of reasons he didn't feel like examining just now.

She shrugged. Maybe he was right. Glancing at the mug, she smiled in satisfaction. It was white again. With a flourish, she placed the mug on the counter and pushed it in front of him. "He likes us to bring our friends with us."

A hint of amusement crossed his lips. "So is that what I am now? A friend?"

She supposed it was as good a label for him as any. *Resident-pain-in-the-butt* just didn't have the same ring to it as *friend* did, although in this case, this was a more accurate assessment.

"Yeah," she agreed after a long moment, "a friend. You don't have to be here," she told him. "You could be home, catching up on the rest of your life—provided you have one."

The coffee was ready. He poured it into the mug and took it black and steaming. Sawyer allowed himself a long sip. He didn't care for the coda she'd added. Because, strictly speaking, other than when he went off fishing by himself twice a year, he had no life, no hobbies that spoke to him, nothing that made him glad for a few days off. He was, first, last and always, a cop. Nothing else mattered; nothing else made sense to him. The rest was just dead time until he could get back to work.

He didn't like her insinuation that there was something wrong with that. She, of all people, should know better.

"Being a cop *is* my life," he informed her tersely. "I like solving puzzles. Like being a cop," he emphasized, "doing cop things."

"Yeah, you'll fit right in tomorrow," she told him with a smile. "That's how they all feel about their careers." She was careful to call it that and not a job, knowing the latter would be taken as an insult. A job was what saw you from paycheck to paycheck. A career was something you poured your heart into. "The only difference being is that they do it for themselves and their families, as well. You know, protect and serve, that kind of thing."

As she talked, Janelle pulled the pins out of her hair. It flowed down around her shoulders now. He'd seen her do it enough times now not to have it capture his train of thought the way it did. But for some reason, he couldn't draw his eyes away. Couldn't remember what he was saying, or even *if* he was saying anything at all.

Maybe it was the way the light glinted in her hair, he wasn't sure. All he knew was that his thoughts had gone off the track, along with his tongue.

"Yeah," he echoed, not really sure what he was agreeing to, except that it seemed safe enough.

"So why do you read Shakespeare?" she asked him suddenly. When he didn't answer, she tried to guess at his reason. "Trying to infuse a little beauty into what you see as a predominantly gritty world?"

"Something like that. Keeps my mind sharp. Occupied."

He should be reading now, Sawyer thought. Because he really needed to occupy his mind, keep it from wandering and his urges from growing. For some reason, being with her tonight felt as if he were sitting on a huge percolator that was going to, at any second, announce that it was through brewing and ready for the next step.

Janelle realized that she hadn't heard what he'd said so much as felt his words along her skin. She'd been watching his mouth the entire time he'd been attempting to speak. There was absolutely no reason to feel suddenly so drawn to him. To feel as if her small apartment were growing smaller. Tightening around the two of them.

And yet…

Okay, she thought, this was wrong, all wrong. She needed to leave, withdraw. Retreat into her room and shut the door until whatever was going on here with her passed and she came back to her senses.

Retreat had a very bad sound to it. It was too much like giving up. And she wasn't one to give up.

Give up what? her mind demanded. This wasn't a territory war. What the hell was going on with her? Why did she have this sudden urge to discover what his mouth would feel like against hers?

This hadn't come out of the blue. If she were really honest with herself, she'd have to admit that this was days in the making. Her insides had been tumbling around like a washing machine for the last few days every time she was anywhere close to him. Even in court, her razor-like sharpness had dulled and it had taken concentration to keep focused. Because she knew he was in the courtroom and she wanted to impress him. Like some adolescent cheerleader executing intricate cheers for the captain of the football team.

No, Sawyer would have never been captain of the football squad. He wouldn't have even been on the team. He wasn't a joiner. But man, he did rattle her teeth. Right down to her core.

Make him go home, her mind pleaded. *Before you beg him to stay.*

"Oh," she mumbled. "Do you want to work on what

we know? About the case," she added, stumbling over her own tongue. "I could send out for pizza—"

He shook his head. He'd had his fill of pizza. "Chinese."

Janelle inclined her head. "Okay, Chinese. We'll see how far we get."

That was exactly what he was afraid of, he thought as he sat back on the stool, nursing the already cooling mug of coffee between his hands.

"Probably not too far," he speculated, only hoping that, on the level that hit closest to home, he was right.

Janelle went over the evidence against Marco's son for what felt like the umpteenth time, except now, she did it for Sawyer's benefit. They had the testimony of Sammy Martinez, a convicted felon who had come forward without being coerced and offered to give up information as to Anthony Wayne's wrongdoings in exchange for having a few years shaved off his sentence. Not exactly a sterling witness, except that what he had told them turned out to be true.

Anthony Wayne's cover, that of being a premed student who was in his senior year, had been completely blown. When the police were sent in with a warrant to search his off-campus apartment, they had found enough cocaine to rule out even the heaviest of recreational use.

"Thereby bringing him up on charges of having an illegal substance with intent to sell," she concluded.

Why didn't it feel right anymore? If Wayne hadn't approached her, if she didn't know her own connection to the man, would she even be giving the case a second thought? It would be a slam dunk.

Maybe too easy a slam dunk, the devil's advocate within her pointed out.

She and Sawyer were in the living room, with containers of Chinese food spread out and opened on the coffee table. She was on the floor against the table while he sat opposite her, on the sofa. Her neck began to protest having to look up at him.

"And this is supposed to be a way of controlling the father," he recounted.

"Right." She subtly moved her head from side to side. Her neck made a small cracking sound, relieving the tension. "Except I'm not sure how—I can see it as a threat," she explained quickly, "warning Wayne that if he doesn't play ball, his kid gets set up and sent away to prison. But that part's already done. Where's the leverage?"

"The leverage is getting him convicted," Sawyer declared as he thought the matter through. His voice became firmer. "Think about it. This kid gets sent up, and if he's the 'good son' that Marco claims he is, he's not going to last that long in prison." Sawyer looked at her. "Do you have any idea what they do to fresh meat in prison?"

Janelle shivered. Things shouldn't be this way, but they were. She couldn't even allow her mind to go there. It was too awful. "I know."

"Once Wayne gives in, things turn around. The informant can conveniently 'disappear.'" Dragging a carton over to him, he looked in, trying to remember if this was what he'd ordered. "Then pressing charges might get dicey."

But like he said, that would require Wayne backing off. Submitting to someone else's authority. She couldn't see the man doing it. "I don't know. Marco didn't look particularly nervous to me—"

Sawyer dipped his chopsticks into the container and came out with a small ball of rice that promptly fell back into the carton as he tried to get it into his mouth. He muttered a curse, then glanced in her direction.

"These people didn't get to where they were by being jumpy. Marco will play it down to the wire, putting his money on you, so to speak," he added. "If you don't come through, he'll take matters into his own hands." It was a sure thing. Unlike his getting any dinner tonight if he used chopsticks, Sawyer thought.

"And kill the informant."

He nodded. "And kill the informant."

"I'll tell Woods he should have the guard doubled." She was thinking out loud now, tossing out anything that occurred to her. All the while she was trying not to laugh as she watched Sawyer's attempts at scoring food. Nice to know he wasn't perfect. "Tripled if necessary."

"Doesn't matter if you use all the king's horses and all the king's men," he told her. "Wayne'll find a way. He's got a long reach." Disgusted, Sawyer temporarily retired the uncooperative chopsticks. "Did anyone dust the cocaine bags they found in Wayne junior's apartment for prints?"

To her knowledge, cocaine bags weren't generally

dusted for prints. Something about the substance inside making it difficult to get clear prints. But Janelle thumbed through the records. First pass showed no mention of dusting for prints. "Not that I can see. Why?"

"Stands to reason that if these were Tony's bags, his prints should be on at least some, if not all, of them. If they're not there, then they were wiped clean. Why? Unless they were planted."

She grinned. Why had something so simple escaped her? "Good point," she agreed eagerly. She made a notation to herself to call the lab first thing in the morning. "I never thought of that," she admitted. She saw him reach for the chopsticks again. The man was nothing if not stubborn. "Why don't you use a fork?" she suggested. "You've been playing with those chopsticks all evening and you're just getting frustrated, not to mention probably hungry."

"I'm not getting frustrated," he snapped, his tone edgy.

"Right. I forgot. That's your usually cheerful voice." Not about to let the matter drop, Janelle got up off the floor and sat down on the couch beside him. "Watch," she instructed.

She held up her right hand and demonstrated how to work the two long sticks that had been sent along with the take-out order.

"Okay, now you," she said, turning over the chopsticks to him. Janelle pressed her lips together, desperately trying to hold back a laugh as he sent several grains of rice flying through the air. Along with several more choice words. "Not quite."

"No kidding, Sherlock," he bit off.

His mood was getting worse. Since he was going out of his way to help her, she decided to try to be encouraging about this. People always worked better with encouragement.

"Almost, though," she coaxed. "Here, hold it like this." She took his hand and inserted first one chopstick and then the other. "One is stationary," she told him. "Only one stick is supposed to move." She showed him again with her own set. "Like this." Then she dropped the two she was holding and started to mold his fingers around his set.

She was too damn close, he thought. Janelle was practically sitting on his side, definitely fitting into the curve of his body. Her scent seemed to be all around him, like an invisible bubble. Sweet, heady. Tantalizing.

Sawyer shook his head to clear it. He was having a great deal of difficulty concentrating on the chopsticks. Or the hunger that supposedly only existed in his belly. That was swiftly fading away. There was another, much more overpowering hunger taking its place. It vibrated through him like an entity that desperately needed excising.

To his knowledge, there was only one way to do that.

Swallowing a raw curse, he dropped the annoying chopsticks and turned his attention to the even more annoying woman. The woman who had been traipsing through his head at unconventional moments, at inconvenient times. Making him crazy.

She felt his eyes on her. Not the chopsticks, but her. Her breath stood still in her throat as she waited. And hoped.

Burying his hands in her hair, Sawyer brought her face toward his and kissed her. Kissed her with all the hunger currently ricocheting throughout his soul.

And went on kissing her.

Rather than end, the kiss built and continued. Continued so much that it fed the fire that had been burning within him for a while now. The fire he'd hoped to somehow put out.

No such luck.

Especially not after he'd made his connection. From Janelle's response, this was not one-sided, and he was relieved. At the same time, her eagerness made it harder for him to step back, to break contact.

And walk away.

But there was no resistance, no signal that he was to back off, to stop. Instead, he was met with a passion that almost swallowed him whole. Janelle wasn't just there for the ride or simply on the receiving end, she was pushing forward.

And kissing him back with feeling.

Something snapped inside of him. The last of his resistance crumbled. He pulled her closer into his arms. Closer against him. Absorbing her warmth, her desire, and making it his own.

He was breaking every single damn rule he'd ever made for himself. He had no idea what came over him, or why. There wasn't anything to point to, no trauma to try to blot out, no anniversary that had dug a pit in his gut or made him feel less than whole. It was her, all her. If anything, she made him feel like a person again. All the numb extremities were no longer numb. Maybe from the moment he'd first laid eyes on her, something about her roused him. Maybe that was why he'd felt this antagonism toward her. It was his own self-preservation mechanism kicking in. Trying to save him.

From what?

From this all-consuming pleasure that was rampaging through him like a gaggle of wild gypsies? No, save him from the aftermath of this. Because there would be an aftermath. Consequences to face. Pipers to pay and all that other garbage. He'd done it before. Once.

He didn't care. All he wanted right now was to feel this happening. To feel, for the first time, as if he were alive and not just on some damn automatic pilot whenever he was away from any life-or-death situation.

That was it. Life or death. Like all the other situations when he'd felt alive, on his game, alert, with adrenaline running full steam ahead through him.

His breathing grew shorter as the demands of his body grew more urgent. Deepening the kiss, he swept his hands over her body, molding her to him, assuring himself that he wasn't just hallucinating all this.

Janelle couldn't remember the last time she'd made love. The last time she'd been with a man. It didn't matter. It didn't count. Heaven help her, this counted. She couldn't pull enough air in her lungs. Her breathing grew shorter as the magnitude of sensations grew larger.

She didn't remember being undressed, could only vaguely remember ripping clothing off him. It was as if lightning chased her, urging her to make the most of this before the storm suddenly left. That was what this felt like. A storm. A storm that wrapped itself around her and pulled her into the very heart of it.

This detective who moved like smoke through a room knew how to make his presence known when he wanted to. He left his mark on her. On all of her. Branding her with his lips as well as his hands, bringing her up to climaxes with the pass of his tongue, the skill of his hands. Finding secret places along her body that greeted him with joy, places she hadn't even realized could offer these kinds of responses.

He was making her crazy.

She found herself digging her nails into him, arching up to absorb the full sensation, the full weight of his body along hers. She bit down on her lower lip to keep from crying out when he brought her up to a full explosion.

Panting, she wiggled down beneath him, her silent urging clear. She wanted them to come together, to be together in the full sense of the word, before she completely ran out of energy.

She felt his smile against her mouth.

They made love quickly, furiously, as if to outrun common sense and the taboos that would have, *should have,* kept them apart. All that mattered was the end goal. The wild, ecstatic climax that would, and did, wipe out everything that was dark and ugly and sad from their lives.

At least for as long as it lasted.

As she slowly came back to earth, she realized Sawyer was holding her to him. Like a lover, not a stranger who'd been caught up in this mysterious whirlwind along with her. It made the euphoria last a little longer.

* * *

"If I'd known that would be your reaction to a clue, I would have asked about the fingerprints a long time ago," Sawyer commented.

He tucked his arm under his head, trying his best to sound removed. Glib. He stared up at her ceiling because he didn't want to see the disapproval he thought might be forming on her face.

She turned toward him, her hair tickling the side of his cheek as she faced him. Her heart was still racing. But there was something more. A radiance that she couldn't contain. She hugged it to her and made the very most of it. Because something this splendid couldn't last long.

"You have an interesting way of guarding a body, Detective."

"Something new I'm trying out," he deadpanned. "Although it was a little fast," he admitted, glancing at his watch. "A lot fast, actually," he amended.

Her eyes widened. She could feel her body warming all over again. "There's a longer, slower version?"

Sawyer laughed and found himself combing his fingers through her hair, moving it away from her face.

Found himself wanting to kiss her again. "Yes."

"Show me," she coaxed, her voice low, husky, throbbing with a myriad of emotions she had no idea how to deal with, other than to allow them to exist.

This was just a release, she told herself, trying not to set herself up for the disappointment she knew had to follow. This was just a way to knock off a little tension, nothing more.

More, a small voice inside her head echoed.

Sawyer looked at her for a long moment. "You're sure?"

Adrenaline began to build all over again. "I'm sure."

She watched as a smile spread along his lips, taking over all of him. Threading itself into her. Binding her to him.

She raised her arms and welcomed him back.

The next minute, she'd crossed over again to a place where there were no clocks, no judgments, nothing but feelings and needs. She would have wept for joy—if she weren't suddenly so very busy.

Chapter 13

There'd been a few times in his life when he'd felt awkward. But he had always managed to mask his feelings and appear to the world the way he always did. Confident. Because he had the kind of face people associated with someone in control, who set the pace rather than followed it, no one ever thought anything could make Sawyer feel awkward. Men like Sawyer Boone did not feel awkward, or uncomfortable. That was for other mortals, whose self-confidence depended on and were built upon outside sources.

Sawyer had always been his own man.

That did not, however, negate the fact that deep down, Sawyer was currently experiencing one of those rare, unsettling moments when he did feel awkward.

Because this time had been so different from the other times when he had made love with a woman. His life, before Allison had come into it and after she had left it, was marked with couplings. With sex, not feelings. With physical attraction, not emotional bonding.

He'd had more than his share of women, although when it came to relationships, not counting Allison, his score was still at zero. Which was where he liked it. He purposely avoided women like Janelle because he didn't want to be in a situation where a relationship could exist. He'd been there once. The pain involved was far too great to risk again.

Which was why he didn't know what the hell he'd been doing last night.

Morning found him alone in the spare bedroom, the tangled sheets beneath him the only testimony that last night had not been a figment of his imagination. That and the hum he still felt along his body.

He could swear if he took in a deep breath, he could still smell her. The scent of her hair, her skin.

He needed to pull himself together, he thought, before their paths crossed this morning. Before he had to face her—and say what? Last night was great, but today's today and we don't look back?

Biting back a curse, Sawyer sat up and scrubbed his hands over his face. Where the hell had his judgment been last night? Or his brain, for that matter?

It had all gone to hell, that's where. And so would he, for what he'd done. If he didn't go there first class, one of the Cavanaughs would undoubtedly send him there.

There was a knock on his door. Muscles all along his upper torso stiffened.

"Sawyer?" Janelle's voice came through the door.

He couldn't gauge her mood from the single word, but he braced himself, just in case. He instinctively knew that she wasn't the kind of woman who engaged in one-night stands or flings. Which made his situation all the worse.

"Yeah?"

"You decent?"

He could have sworn he detected a smile. Sawyer didn't know if that made things worse or better. "Not since I was fifteen."

Her laugh, like a much needed shot of brandy on a cold night, burrowed right into him, settling around his belly and nesting there. Arousing him.

He didn't want this, he told himself. Didn't need this. Didn't know what the hell to *do* with this.

The doorknob turned. Sawyer drew the sheet around his middle. They'd made love last night, but this morning, he was looking to return to the status quo. That didn't include either one of them being naked.

Janelle stuck her head in and seemed mildly surprised to find him still in bed. That made two of them, given that he was ordinarily such a light sleeper. He should have woken up the second she'd started to slip out of bed.

"We need to get going," she told him.

He started to get up, then stopped. That naked thing again. He'd have to wait until she left the room. Her words played themselves over in his head, registering this time. "I thought you said you didn't want a body-guard anymore."

"Maybe I was wrong," she allowed. If someone was out to control Wayne through his son, and she seemed to be the most likely candidate to challenge the evidence, then eliminating her from the scene, as Sawyer had pointed out, would be to that person's benefit. "But I'm not talking about you being my bodyguard. We're supposed to be on our way to Uncle Andrew's house." She saw the dark brown eyebrows draw together in a vacant scowl. Funny, she never noticed how sexy that scowl was before. "Breakfast, remember?"

The former police chief's visit last night came back to him in broken bits. Everything that had transpired in the last twelve hours had taken a back seat to their lovemaking.

He stared at her now, not a little stunned. "You're se-rious?"

She wasn't exactly sure how to take that. She decided not to feel slighted, or to allow herself to make anything more of last night than it having been the most teeth-jarring experience of her life. If she wanted it to be more, to mean more to him, she wasn't going to let herself go there. She'd known the kind of man he was at the outset. And he wasn't a nester.

But he was engaged once. Loved someone enough not to ride out of town and into the sunset.

She shut out the voice in her head. "I might not be, but he is. I've learned you never turn down a personal invitation from Uncle Andrew." Her mouth curved. "There are consequences."

He blew out a breath, feeling trapped. More by his own reactions than the so-called command performance. "Look, if this is because of last night—"

"It is." Then, before he could protest or begin a rebuttal, she added, "He was here last night, remember? Told me to bring you." She knew that wasn't what Sawyer was referring to, but at the moment she wasn't up to hearing him say *It was just one of those things. Suck it up, honey.* "I believe the words *tomorrow morning* were specifically used." She spread her hands wide. "Well, guess what? It's tomorrow morning."

He groaned. Andrew Cavanaugh might be the former chief of police, but he was still related to half the police force, not to mention the current chief of detectives. Deliberately ignoring the man's invitation was not a wise move. Not if he wanted to stay here. And although he'd told himself that one place was as good or bad as another, he'd put down roots here. He didn't want to leave just yet.

"Give me a few minutes."

She nodded, then paused by the door to look over her shoulder. He was still sitting there. "Hustle."

With that, she closed the door. And made sure she was on the other side of it. No matter what she wanted to the contrary.

The second the back door opened, the warmth found Sawyer, surrounding him like a comforting embrace.

It was a combination of warm air generated by so many bodies in a limited amount of space, and warmth generated by the actual people who comprised those bodies.

Voices rose, shouting greetings and teasing remarks, all aimed at the woman who had entered the country kitchen just ahead of him. To his surprise, several calls of greeting were sent in his direction, as well. Sawyer recognized none of the voices although some faces were vaguely familiar from the police department.

His eyes quickly swept over the crowd, making assessments. For the most part, Cavanaugh men had black hair and sky-blue eyes. Their female counterparts were blondes with green eyes. All except for the redhead left of center. They were all dynamic. The children present seemed to be running on self-recharging triple-A batteries.

Sawyer could feel himself withdrawing.

For the most part, he'd done undercover work in the last three years. That kept him out of the general loop. On occasion, he would be summoned and told to come into police headquarters. But usually he was left on his own, and he liked it that way.

Except for the brief period when he'd been engaged to Allison, he'd been an outsider for most of his life. That's what made him so good at what he'd done up until now. Blending in. Being invisible. Observing was second nature to an outsider because there was nothing else to take up his time.

"We left you a space," Andrew informed him, as if he'd been expecting him to come all along.

The older man pointed out two seats at the table he'd

had custom-made to accommodate his ever-expanding family. When he'd first left the department, shortly after his wife's disappearance, there'd been a regular table to grace the kitchen. But as his cooking skills had improved and his desire to have his family around him had increased, he'd had a table made to accommodate them.

Now, because his family had more than doubled in size, there were three tables placed as close together as possible and extending from the kitchen through the family room into the dining room. Physical walls had been moved so that emotional ones were never given an opportunity to go up.

Janelle looked around. She hadn't been here in several weeks, since before Sawyer had appeared on the scene. The extra work had drastically cut into her free time. She realized just how much she'd missed these people who were so dear to her. These people she had very nearly, in her anger and hurt, given up.

Her mouth curved. Showed her that even she could be an idiot.

Right now it looked as if half the family was missing, she assessed. Only one of her brothers, Dax, with his wife, Brenda, and their infant daughter, was at the table. The rest of the spaces were filled by four of Andrew's five children, Callie, Shaw, Clay and Teri, and their spouses and assorted children. Rayne and her husband were missing. As were her cousin Patrick and his wife, Maggie. But Patience, the lone redhead, and her husband Brady were there. Their eyes met and she nodded at her cousin.

The noise level in the house was almost overwhelming, but it faded into the background as she made eye contact with the one man she'd been hoping to find here.

He was already on his feet, crossing to her in long strides, his face a wreath of smiles that simultaneously made her happy and weepy.

"You came," Brian said, his voice low. She heard him despite the din.

"I came," Janelle whispered.

The next moment, she was enveloped in her father's strong arms. Arms, she recalled, that had created a safe haven for her more than once when she was growing up.

When she glanced over toward her uncle, still locked in her father's embrace, she saw that Andrew was unabashedly wiping away tears with the heel of his hand. The man had never been ashamed of his emotions.

"So," he said loudly after clearing his throat. "Anyone tell me what goes with sentiment?"

"Syrup," Callie, his oldest daughter, cheerfully declared. The next moment, she was lifting up a serving platter and offering it to the newest face at their table. "Pancakes, Sawyer?"

"Let the man have some strong coffee first," Clay, her younger brother and Teri's twin, cut in. "We're not exactly the easiest bunch to take first thing in the morning."

"If he can put up with Janelle first thing in the morning—or any time," Dax told his cousin, "then everything else is a cakewalk."

"Sit, boy," Andrew instructed, his hand on Sawyer's shoulder, gently but firmly urging him down. "Let me fill your plate."

Before Sawyer could point out that he had no plate to fill, one was placed in front of him by a slender blonde who appeared to be somewhat older than the other women in the room. By the way she looked at Andrew, he judged that she had to be the man's wife.

"Now you can fill it," Rose Cavanaugh told her husband after smiling at Sawyer.

Same old family, Janelle thought, taking a seat next to Sawyer. She'd lost count how many times they'd all gone through this with other strangers who'd joined the group. Most of those, she recalled, had gone on to become permanent fixtures at the gatherings, appreciating them even more than those who'd been born into the family.

That wasn't the case with Sawyer, she reminded herself. His position here was just temporary. Maybe even a one-time thing.

Even as she told herself that, a sadness materialized out of nowhere, settling into the pit of her stomach.

She was just hungry, nothing more. Janelle helped herself to a serving of scrambled eggs and toast. She slanted a glance toward Sawyer. Maybe it was time she threw him a lifeline.

"Okay, let me run through the names for you," she offered. "You already know my uncle Andrew and my dad." Both men nodded at him. She twisted around in her seat to look at the woman who had just given them both silverware. "That lovely lady is my aunt Rose. My brother, Dax and his wife, Brenda," she said, gesturing toward the couple in the middle of the next table. "And these are my cousins." She rattled off each of their names, plus the names of their spouses and children, as she indicated each in turn in quick, staccato fashion.

Sawyer felt as if he were swimming in alphabet soup long before she was finished.

The woman in the middle of the next table smiled at him as if she knew exactly what he was going through. "Don't worry," she told him with a wink. "There's no quiz at the end. This time," she qualified.

"Hey, no flirting with Janelle's bodyguard," Dax protested, pretending to be indignant with his wife. "It'll throw him off his game."

"And being with Janelle won't?" Teri wanted to know.

"You've got a point," Dax acknowledged with a nod. He turned to Brenda. "Pass the powdered sugar, honey."

On her way back to the coffee urn, Rose paused by Sawyer's chair and inclined her head. "Yes, they're always like this," she confided in a pseudo-low voice. "When they're here. Out in the field is another story." Straightening, she smiled at the lot of them. There was no missing the pride in her eyes. If Andrew was the patriarch, then she was the matriarch, if belatedly so. The position was not taken lightly.

He was surprised that Rose Cavanaugh had stopped to say anything to him. Was she just assuming what his reaction to the others was, or was his expression not as stony or unreadable as he would have liked?

* * *

Since this was a command performance before the former police chief, he'd intended to simply eat and keep to himself. But he discovered that it wasn't only the best laid plans of mice and men that went astray, but also those belonging to former undercover policemen. Despite the fact that a great deal of conversation already flew back and forth across the tables, questions were fired at him, as well. Questions that continued to hang in the air until he answered them.

Against his will, Sawyer found himself drawn into first the peripheral conversations, then into the main discussions, as well. Before he knew it, despite an active attempt at resistance, he was embedded in the threads of a typical Cavanaugh breakfast. And discovered that it really wasn't so bad after all.

"Well, you survived," Janelle said as they walked back to their respective vehicles a little more than an hour later.

Fishing out his car keys, he spared her a glance. "Did you think I wouldn't?"

She wasn't about to tell him that she'd held her breath more than once during the course of the morning, watching him more closely than she'd ever watched anyone else at the table before. It had been worse than the first time she'd pleaded a case in court. She'd even felt nervous for him, although he'd looked just fine throughout the whole thing.

"No, I knew you would." In fact, Sawyer could

handle himself well anywhere. "But I think you might have had your doubts."

He shrugged carelessly as they made their way around to the front driveway. "Hell of a lot of noise going on in there." He paused to give her a significant look. "And prying."

"They're cops," she reminded him. "They ask questions. And theirs were meant in the best possible way," she added, absolving her family in one giant swoop. "We Cavanaughs care about the people we come across." The second the words were out, they echoed back to her. Janelle smiled.

Sawyer paused to look at her for a long, scrutinizing moment. "You over it?"

"Over what?"

He nodded back toward the house. Someone was watching them. Someone short. The curtain in the living room was pushed back, and he could make out a small figure at the window. Definitely one of the kids. "Being mad because you were kept in the dark."

Janelle laughed as she opened the door on the driver's side. "I suppose I am at that." Her face softened as a fond expression came over it. "They're a hard bunch to stay mad at." About to leave, she hesitated, then turned to look at him. Awkward or not, this had to be said, had to be put out in the open. "Look, I don't want you to think that this was anything more than just bringing you over because Uncle Andrew asked me to. You're not being absorbed, or indoctrinated. They're a bunch of nice people. Getting to know them is a good thing. It's a big police department. You can never tell when you might need one of them."

God, was that really her, stumbling over her own tongue like that? She'd always been so good, so succinct at stating what she thought. Now she sounded like someone having trouble rubbing two sentences together.

With effort, Janelle tried again. "I guess what I'm trying to say is that last night came with no strings."

"Good to know," he said. For reasons he couldn't fathom, her assurances did not make him feel better. If anything, they made him feel more restless. He paused, about to get into his car, which was parked behind hers. "What if, just for the sake of argument…" His voice trailed off. He couldn't even put the situation into hypothetical terms without feeling the urge to back away.

And yet, when he did back away, there was this urge to retrace his steps again.

Was this what going insane was like?

Janelle stared at him, suddenly reading between the lines. Fear and joy raced through her. So why did she feel like smiling?

"Should the need arise, strings can be obtained at the checkout counter," she informed him flippantly and followed it up with a grin. "I'll see you around, Detective," she said as she got in behind the steering wheel.

She saw him in her rearview mirror all the way to the county building. He followed close enough behind so that no other vehicle got between them.

Sawyer was taking the job he no longer had seriously,

and it should have annoyed her. Should have, but didn't. She admitted she liked not being alone.

But the moment she turned into the parking lot where she worked, Janelle lost sight of Sawyer's dark blue sports car. Had he just escorted her in and then taken off?

Janelle vaguely recalled that Sawyer had said something about taking some time off, but she hadn't thought he was really serious. Apparently he was, she thought as she scanned the wide open area.

The man was full of surprises, she mused, locking her car. And none so great as the one she'd received last night. It had been a double whammy. He'd surprised her and she, in turn, had surprised herself.

Thinking it over, she decided that a prolonged abstinence didn't have anything to do with her reaction to Sawyer. *Sawyer* had something to do with her reaction to Sawyer.

The very thought of him now sent warm, tingling shivers all up and down her spine, stealing away her very breath.

Idiot, she thought. Bringing him to her uncle's table notwithstanding, if anyone had ever struck her as definitely *not* the settling down type, it was Detective Sawyer Boone. He was even more of a loner than her cousin Teri's husband, Hawk, had been when they'd first met him. And that was saying a great deal.

Hurrying toward the front steps of the building, Janelle almost went flying as her heel caught on something. Her hand flew out and she stopped her fall by bracing herself on the hood of a black Honda.

Well, that had been fun, she thought darkly.

Janelle checked her shoe to make sure the heel wasn't broken. Still bracing herself against the hood of the Honda, she looked down as she put her shoe back on. She expected, if anything, to find a rock or a broken piece of asphalt. The summer had been hot, causing the asphalt to become more pliable. Potholes had resulted. Several pockmarked the lot with their accompanying loose pieces of asphalt.

But what she saw, almost kicked under the car she was leaning on, was neither a rock nor a piece of asphalt. It was a cell phone.

Chapter 14

Janelle stooped down to pick up the cell phone. It was a little dirty, but didn't appear to be damaged. Undoubtedly it had fallen out of someone's purse or pocket as they'd gotten out of the car and then been kicked around at least once.

Somebody was going to be very unhappy to find their phone was missing. She knew more than a few people who felt as if their entire life was stored on the tiny microchip that resided within their phones. She hadn't gotten to that stage yet, but she would be lost without her PDA.

Flipping the cell phone open, Janelle checked to see if the unit was still operational, or if she'd accidentally kicked the life right out of it.

The screen lit up like the face of a child who was happy to see her.

Relieved, she slipped the cell phone into her oversize black purse that on occasion also doubled as a briefcase. Okay, anything else involving the phone was going to have to be put on hold for a little while. Right now, she was running late and not at all comfortable about waltzing in after nine. Being late for any reason went against her own rules.

When she stepped off the elevator, she found that no one was around to notice she was late. Woods was in a meeting where he'd been since eight, according to his secretary, and Kleinmann was still on the East Coast. The other assistants to the A.D.A. were all going about their business, noses to grindstones and arms laden with files, oblivious to anything but their own personal misery.

Janelle lost no time in getting down to work and spent the first hour working on other cases. But as the second hour began its rotation around the clock, Janelle's attention started shifting toward the case that was no longer her concern. She started by doing some checking into Anthony Wayne's background, wading through transcripts and any public and not-so-public records she could get her hands on.

The fact that she was checking out her half brother was not lost on her. Everything about the case screamed conflict of interest.

It also, she realized, screamed *quick*.

Less than half a day had gone by and she already had the distinct impression that the prosecuting side of the case was so eager for conviction that corners were slashed and shortcuts were raced across. She leaned back in her chair, staring at the latest report she'd pulled up on the screen. Something just didn't feel right. She was beginning to believe that Marco had been straight with her.

Just as Marco had maintained, his son's record, until the raid that had led to Tony's arrest, had been spotless. A straight-A premed student on his way to becoming a doctor, Anthony Wayne could not have had dealings further away from his father's world if he'd tried.

Or if Marco had tried.

Rocking in her chair, she laced her fingers together, thinking. If the younger Wayne was so blameless, where had the drugs come from? They had found over a kilo's worth divided up into small nickel bags. The entire stash had been hidden under the mattress in the spare bedroom. Had they been planted as Marco maintained? Or was Anthony, with his heretofore exemplary life, the perfect cover for drug dealing? And why had there been a raid just then, with all of this just sitting there, waiting to be found?

Janelle shook her head. Thinking. Seemed like a hell of a coincidence from where she was sitting. And although those did occur in life, she was leaning more toward conspiracy.

She glanced at the name of the arresting officer and decided that maybe it was time for her to have a little chat of her own with Detective Conway.

Grabbing her purse, she left a quick note on her desk that she was taking a couple of hours personal time, in case Woods ever came looking for her.

As she made her way out into the corridor, she bumped into Mariel. Ordinarily the picture of cheerfulness, the dark-haired assistant looked distraught and somewhat lost. She mumbled a belated, "Excuse me," and started to walk away.

Placing her hand on the other woman's shoulder, Janelle stopped her. "Is something wrong, Mariel?" She looked as if she'd just lost three cases in a row and was up for performance review.

Mariel only shook her head. The smile that appeared on her lips had been forced there.

"Just overworked," she answered, then added, "and I think I'm coming down with something," following it up with a sniffle.

Because of the intense, long hours that were often required, Janelle had learned not too far into the job that it paid to keep an assortment of pharmaceutical products on hand.

"Top side drawer in my desk," Janelle instructed, pointing toward her office. "Help yourself to anything you need."

A spasmodic smile came and went swiftly. "Thanks." With a nod, Mariel hurried off.

In the opposite direction, Janelle noted. She was about to point that out, then thought better of it. The assistant didn't look as if she wanted to be corrected and Janelle had a detective to see.

Twenty minutes later, she walked out of the elevator onto the fourth floor of the police department. Janelle had a general idea where Narcotics was located and headed in that direction.

Her mouth dropped open when she discovered Sawyer there ahead of her. Talking to the man she had come to see.

When Sawyer turned to look over his shoulder and saw her standing there, he didn't appear to be the least surprised. Instead, he merely nodded, as if he'd expected her all along.

From the sound of it, he was wrapping his conversation up.

"Thanks for the information, Conway," he said, getting to his feet.

The other man grunted in response, then turned back to typing something on his keyboard. If he was aware of her presence behind him, Conway gave no indication.

Janelle was about to say something to the other detective, but Sawyer quickly commandeered her arm and led her away from the small cubicle where Detective James Conway was sitting. Very deliberately, he directed her back the way she had just entered.

"Excuse me?" she demanded, pulling her arm free. Just because they'd slept together didn't give Sawyer the right to dictate what she did and where she went. "I need to talk to him."

He took hold of her arm again to hold her in place. "You don't have to." Janelle's eyes widened at his gall. "I already did."

And what, he was the last word in everything? "Maybe I want to ask him something you didn't cover."

He looked at her knowingly. "Like why he and the others raided Anthony Wayne's off-campus apartment on the exact day that they did?"

Some of her fire went out, but at least he wasn't gloating. "All right, maybe you did ask him the same question I was going to."

He lifted one shoulder in a half shrug. "Great minds—"

"Even a broken clock is right twice a day."

His eyes held hers for a moment. Damn but she had gotten to him. Attempts to shake off her effects didn't seem to be working. He didn't want to get gotten to.

So why are you still hanging around?

He had no answer to give the annoying little voice inside his head. So for now, he ignored it. "Which of us is the broken clock?"

"Never mind that, what did Conway say about why he picked that day to raid Tony Wayne?"

"Just about what I expected him to say," Sawyer told her. He stretched his words out, knowing that it set her off. He had no idea why he liked watching the fire come into her eyes, but he did. "That his information had come via an anonymous tip. It went along with what Sam Martinez said."

"You believe him?"

He'd already checked Conway out. The man was a good cop. No evidence of his ever having been compromised. Not everything was a conspiracy. "No reason not to."

"Did they try to trace the call?"

He shook his head. "The woman didn't stay on the line long enough for them to do that."

Her eyes widened. This was the first she'd heard of a woman placing the call. She'd just naturally assumed it was a man. Which made her as guilty as everyone else when it came to stereotyping and profiling. "A woman?"

"Yeah." He liked the surprise on her face. Liked her face, he thought. He knew he was on dangerous ground here and he was really going to have to watch his step. For his own sake. "According to Conway, she said something about Wayne Jr. supplying her brother and that the kid had overdosed on the stuff, which was why she was calling us. For revenge and so that no other kid could die like her brother did.

"But then she was gone. Conway said she sounded genuine and the department had been trying for a long time to get something on Wayne that would stick."

Janelle pointed out the obvious. "But this is Wayne Jr."

He nodded, indicating that he went along with her thinking. "They figured it was a start." Sawyer took a breath, waiting until the two detectives who were walking down the hall had passed them before he continued. "What are you doing here, anyway? I thought I was the one who was supposed to chase down leads."

She supposed that had been the original division of labor, but she hadn't really been paying that much attention to rules, not when all heaven breaking loose had followed. "I got restless."

To her surprise, Sawyer laughed ruefully, running

his hand along the back of his neck. "Yeah, I know what you mean."

Her eyes met his. And she knew exactly what he was saying. Neither of them was talking about the restlessness that came from dealing with unresolved cases. It was far more basic than that.

Sawyer took a breath, as if making up his mind about something. "You know, we're not that far from my place."

Her eyes narrowed as she tried to absorb the meaning behind the words. "You're inviting me over to your apartment?"

He glanced at his watch. "It's lunchtime."

Janelle took his wrist and held it so that he could see his watch more clearly. It wasn't that late yet. "It's eleven o'clock."

He shrugged as he dropped his hand. "So, make it an early lunch."

She regarded him for a moment, mystified. "You could actually eat after everything that my uncle loaded on your plate?"

His eyes held hers for what seemed like an eternity. "Who said anything about eating?"

This, she told herself, was where she cut the line and ran. Or at least turned on her heel and walked away. This was not a man a woman could build a future with. He was the last word in rootlessness and the sooner she wrapped her mind around that, the better it would be for her.

Knowing this, *believing* this, she was surprised to hear herself say, "You lead, I'll follow in my car."

Sawyer didn't say a word. Not *okay,* not *fine.* Not

even a quick nod of his head. But the grin on his face remained with her the entire short trip from the police station to his modest garden apartment complex.

She was so intent on keeping Sawyer's car in sight, she hardly took note of the route, which was bad. Had she abruptly decided to retrace her steps, she wouldn't have been able to do that without first pulling over to the side in order to examine the road map she kept tucked away in the passenger door.

Although the tips of her fingers felt damp, there were no sudden decisions to turn around and go back. If anything, the anticipation kept building with each tenth of a mile that passed.

Because of the hour, there were a lot of empty spaces in the complex. She passed where he parked his car in order to slip into a space two aisles over.

The moment she pulled up her hand brake, the door on her side opened and Sawyer was pulling her out. Pulling her out of the car and into his arms.

Any protest or pretense at surprise faded in the wake of the heat instantly traveling up and down her body. His mouth covered hers and she found herself melting as she threaded her arms around his neck and kissed him back. Doing what she'd been thinking about doing ever since she had left his bed this morning.

Janelle could feel her body responding, could feel it tightening like an instrument being tuned. Primed. Ready for the concert that was coming.

She didn't remember how she got from the parking

space to his apartment. It was almost as if she had been teleported across the distance. Neither did she remember taking off her clothes or having them removed. One minute, she was standing out in the open beside her car, fully clothed, kissing and being kissed. The next, she was inside his apartment, naked and completely on fire.

They made love faster than she would have ever thought possible. The all-consuming desires that ricocheted through her body all but exploded within what seemed like minutes. He'd gotten her to climax in breathtaking speed.

And when it was over, they did it again. And again. Until neither one could move and they both lay together on the floor, only several feet into the apartment, trying desperately to regulate their breathing or, at the very least, their pulse rate.

Janelle waited for the embarrassment, the regret, to overtake her. Neither made an appearance. Another wave of desire came instead, along with an almost debilitating tenderness that flooded her veins.

She had no idea what to do with it.

Her breathing a tiny bit steadier, she covered her eyes with one of her hands, trying somehow to pull herself together.

"I don't believe I've ever done it that quickly before." Dropping her hand, she turned her head slightly to look at him. "Or that often."

He looked at her, an unreadable expression on his face. "I believe in making the most of my time," he told her softly. Though drolly delivered, the response struck her as funny. So funny that she started to laugh. Once she got started, she couldn't seem to stop. Janelle laughed so hard, she wound up getting hiccups.

"Now see—hic—what you've—hic—done. I'm—hic—supposed to—hic—be in—hic—court this—hic—afternoon." Concern grew as she tried to stop and found she really couldn't. "How—hic—am I—hic—supposed to—hic—ask the—hic—judge for—hic—no remand—hic—like this—hic?"

Sawyer couldn't keep the amusement he felt from showing. But he did his best to appear concerned. "You're right. This is serious." He rolled over onto his stomach, his upper torso half covering hers. "I could try scaring you."

"If this—hic—isn't scary—hic—enough," she said, referring to how quickly they had come together, "I—hic—don't know—hic—what is—hic."

He drew her even closer, so that their breaths mingled along with their heartbeats. "By 'this' you mean making love with me?"

She could feel herself heating again. Longing. Even as her chest kept heaving from the damn hiccups. "Yeah—hic."

"Okay," he said gamely, "then we'll try more of the same."

Before she could protest, he brought his lips down over hers, momentarily stealing her breath away. At first, her hiccups echoed inside his mouth as well as her body. But gradually, as he kissed her over and over again, his hands passing along her flesh, claiming her the way he had before, the hiccups subsided until they finally disappeared altogether.

She felt as if she were spinning out of her own body and into space.

"Does the AMA know about this method?" she murmured the moment his mouth left hers and began to trail along her throat. Her hiccups might have been gone, but her body vibrated like a tuning fork struck against a goblet filled with champagne.

"Haven't had time to notify them," he answered, his breath gliding along her skin, heightening her arousal with every passing second. "You can take the credit for it if you want."

There was only one thing she wanted right now and credit had nothing to do with it.

Janelle had no idea what was going on or why Sawyer had this effect on her. All she knew was that she desperately wanted it to continue for as long as possible. Somehow, in the space of less than twenty-four hours, she had gotten utterly and incredibly hooked on a man she knew was bad for her.

Bad only because she knew that this would end one way. Badly. At least, for her. But it didn't stop her from wanting to be with him. From wanting to make love with him. Over and over again until she expired.

From out of a haze, she heard his voice against her ear. She shivered even as it brought a blanket of warmth with it.

"We've only got fifteen minutes left," Sawyer whispered urgently.

Fifteen minutes. The blink of an eye, or eternity. It all depended on the way it was handled.

"Then we'd better make the most of it," she told him. Before he could digest her words, she pushed him onto his back and began to move along his body. Straddling him, she did her very best to bring him as close to a climax as physically possible before she drew back and retreated.

She did it not once, but three times. When she heard him groan, a wicked, pleasure-filled laugh escaped her lips. It was nice, just this once, to be in control. There was so little of it where he was concerned.

But as she went to move away the third time, Sawyer surprised her as he caught her wrists and pulled her down to him.

"Not this time," he warned. There were sparks in his eyes. She could feel an electrical current pass through her. Holding her fast, Sawyer switched their positions until he was the one on top. And then he proceeded to do things to her that she could only term as sweet agony. Every nerve ending raced up to the surface, eager to take part. To feel.

Sawyer anointed her body with his tongue until she was primed and moist, ready to come apart at the seams.

Poised over her body, his hands joined with hers, he looked down at her, a grin on his face. His eyes teased hers. "Tables are turned, Cavanaugh. Tell me, how does it feel?"

She raised her head. "I won't tell you, I'll show you." The next minute, she stretched as far as she could. Her lips captured his.

It was all the encouragement he needed.

Unable to resist her or the demands slamming

through his body any longer, Sawyer sank down into the heated kiss. After a beat, he parted her legs with his knee. The next moment, they were joined and urgently racing toward the final moment that they had been anticipating. When they reached it, the movement kept it escalating for as long as humanly possible.

Neither wanted it to end. Or to have reality descend before absolutely necessary.

Chapter 15

Very slowly, but faster than she was happy about, the euphoria lifted and receded. Reality arrived to nudge her, however unwillingly, back into her everyday world. At the same moment, strains of "Tara," the theme song from *Gone With the Wind*, intrusively elbowed its way into the atmosphere.

Confused, still a little disoriented, Janelle turned only her head toward Sawyer. "Do you have music that goes on automatically?" He didn't strike her as the type. That kind of scene belonged to a Romeo, something Sawyer definitely was not.

"If I did, it wouldn't be that." Sawyer sat up, listening. At first he thought the music might be coming from a neighboring apartment. But it sounded too close, as if in the same room with them. "That's coming from your purse," he realized. Sawyer frowned. Didn't she recognize her own phone? "That's a hell of a ring tone for your cell phone."

Mixing modesty and pragmatism, Janelle had already slipped on her underwear while Sawyer was trying to determine the origin of the music. Getting to her feet, she grabbed her blouse and punched her arms through the sleeves. She reached for her purse, lying beside her discarded skirt. The theme was still continuing, but who knew for how long.

"That's not my phone."

"Phonesitting?" he guessed as she pulled a cell phone out of the bowels of her purse. The phone looked as if it had been kicked around a bit.

Janelle held her hand up to silence him as she flipped open the cell. "Hello?"

"Mariel?" the voice on the other end was male and sounded uncertain.

"No, I—"

Before she could say another word, or ask anything, the connection went dead. Frowning, she flipped the cover closed again. "Guess that answers that," she commented more to herself than to Sawyer.

"You come with subtitles?" Sawyer asked. She turned around to see that he was behind her and had already pulled on his jeans.

She supposed he deserved an explanation and told him as much as she knew. "I found this phone in the parking lot this morning. I was going to try to find out who it belonged to, but then I got caught up doing things at work and completely forgot about it." She looked at the item in her hand. "The cell phone belongs to Mariel. Collins," she added after a beat.

She could see the name meant absolutely nothing to Sawyer. Why should it?

"She's one of the assistants in the D.A.'s office," Janelle explained. A fragment of a scene played back in her head. "No wonder she looked so upset this morning," she realized. "Mariel was probably looking for her phone."

Picking up her skirt, she was about to step into it when she suddenly paused. Something wasn't right. "Then why didn't she say anything?" Her eyes met Sawyer's. It was obvious to her that he was waiting for her to start making sense. "When I asked her if anything was wrong—because she looked really upset and nervous about something—she said no. Why wouldn't she tell me she was looking for her cell phone? Or ask me if I'd seen it?"

"Maybe because she had something to hide." Slipping on his dark shirt, he began to button it. "Usually when people don't ask for help it's because they don't want any attention drawn to the problem."

"Either that, or they're super macho and have an ego problem."

"Wouldn't know about that," he commented absently. His mind juggling disjointed pieces of the puzzle, Sawyer suddenly stopped buttoning his shirt and took the phone from her. Tapping an icon in the center, he opened the menu screen and began to scroll down.

He looked like a man with a purpose, she thought. "What are you doing? Besides invading privacy," she qualified.

The phone was tiny. His fingers were not. It was difficult getting to the right screen. "Seeing who this Marion—"

"Mariel," Janelle corrected.

"Mariel," he repeated, this time committing the name to memory. "Who this Mariel was making and getting calls from recently."

Janelle made an attempt to look over his shoulder, but he was just too tall and too broad-shouldered. Giving up, she settled for looking at the phone upside down.

"Why would you want to do that?"

He swallowed a curse as he found himself on a screen he didn't want. Going back, he tried again. This time, the icon for recent calls came up. He pressed it and moved on to a menu that gave him a choice between incoming and outgoing.

"To find out what she had to hide."

She thought of Mariel. Glasses of water had more to hide than the mousy woman. "What if there's nothing to hide?"

Sawyer didn't bother shrugging. "Then no harm, no foul." He slanted a glance in her direction. Janelle was, after all, a lawyer and probably very wrapped up in truth, justice and strict guidelines. "I won't tell if you won't."

It was hard to debate a person's right to privacy when she was talking to a man whose shirt was only half-buttoned. But she still couldn't come out and condone what he was doing, so she refrained from commenting on his last words, turned away and finished getting dressed.

"Interesting."

"What is?" she asked despite herself. Dressed, she turned back around to face him. His shirt was still partially open and he looked like one of those brooding heroes who graced the covers of historical romances. She tried not to dwell on that.

"Mariel seems to be calling a particular number quite a lot." He pointed it out to her.

Craning her neck, she looked at the recent history of the calls. There *were* a lot. But that didn't mean anything. "Maybe it's her boyfriend."

He shut the phone and slipped it into his pocket. "Not unless she's going with someone from Charlie Wentworth's house."

The name had her doing a mental double take. She looked at Sawyer sharply, growing wary. Why had he plucked that name out of the air? That was the man Wayne had claimed was behind framing his son. "How would you know his number?"

"My life didn't start the day I took on being your bodyguard," he reminded her. Although, he added silently, there had been a few minutes, like just earlier and last night, when he might have felt tempted to say otherwise. "I worked undercover for three years. Let's just say some of the paths I took led me through organized-crime territory."

"And you remember Wentworth's personal number."

The expression on Sawyer's face negated her doubts. "I've got total recall."

Did that apply to things written down on a page, or to events, as well? She felt a little vulnerable. "Should have warned me earlier."

The smile was small. Its effect was not. "Where's the fun in that?"

She could feel herself responding to the look in his eyes. To him. Janelle struggled to bank down her reactions, but it wasn't easy. "Why would an assistant to the A.D.A. be calling someone like Wentworth?"

"That's the big question," he acknowledged. "But for the time being—" he began buttoning his shirt again "—I think you might have found your leak."

"You found my phone!" Mariel cried when Janelle got directly in front of her in the woman's office and held the cell phone up before her.

Janelle had been in the building less than five minutes. The moment they'd walked in, she'd asked Sawyer to go to the crime lab and check on the tech's progress with finding any fingerprints on the bags of cocaine confiscated in Anthony's apartment. They separated at the front entrance, with her going up to the D.A.'s floor to confront Mariel.

Sawyer hadn't seemed happy with the division of labor, but making him happy wasn't her prime objective at the moment. Finding out what the hell was going on had taken center stage.

"Yes, I did," she replied, studying the young woman

before her. Mariel still looked harmless. Was there some mistake? "You dropped it in the parking lot."

Mariel spread her hand over her chest, sighing dramatically. "You saved my life," she declared, reaching for the cell.

Janelle moved the object just out of reach. "Maybe not. What are you doing with Charlie Wentworth's phone number on your cell?"

She could have sworn Mariel paled just a little. "Who?"

"Oh please, don't insult my intelligence. You're not dumb, Mariel. You know who Charlie Wentworth is. Especially since Woods handed you my chair." She'd felt a pang when she'd heard that the A.D.A. had given her position at the prosecution table to Mariel.

Mariel immediately defended herself. "You withdrew from the case."

"And so should you."

"Why?" she asked nervously.

It was an act, Janelle thought. All of it. The shy looks, the submissive attitude, all an act. Her eyes narrowed. "Because you've been keeping Wentworth apprised of everything that's been going on here regarding Anthony Wayne's case."

The deer-in-the-headlights expression receded. Mariel began straightening the papers on her desk. Her laugh was forced. "Why would I do something like that?"

Leaning over her desk, Janelle put her hand down on the folders Mariel was tidying, forcing the woman to look at her. "You tell me."

Mariel's voice stopped quivering. "The only thing I'm doing is telling Stephen that you've lost your mind." She began to leave, but Janelle put her hand on her shoulder, stopping her. She shrugged it off. "You need some time off to get back to your A game, Janelle."

"While you tamper with evidence and get Anthony Wayne convicted for something he didn't do for some reason I can't fathom yet? I don't think so."

A flash of anger flared in Mariel's deep brown eyes. "You're making a mistake, Janelle."

"You're the one who made a mistake," Janelle corrected. "But I'm going to Woods with this." Janelle held up the cell phone. "Next time you try to put one over on someone, remember to get a disposable cell phone."

With that, Janelle spun on her heel and was about to walk out. But she never made it out the door because Mariel blocked her way. The weapon in the other woman's hand was pointed straight at Janelle's stomach.

"Where did you get that?" Janelle asked.

"I have my ways," Mariel replied smugly. "And I don't know about the phone being disposable, but now you're going to have to be." Mariel shook her head, her dark hair shimmying around her face. "I wish you'd kept out of it, Janelle." There was a note of genuine regret in her voice. "I liked you."

Janelle needed to keep the woman talking until someone came in. Or until Mariel came to her senses. "No need to use past tense, Mariel. I'm still here."

"Not for long." Her eyes trained on Janelle, Mariel felt around along the back of her chair until she found her purse. "We're going to go to lunch together. And then only one of us is coming back."

Her hands raised slightly and, eyeing the weapon warily, Janelle still made no move to leave the office. "I already went out to lunch."

"You'll go out again," Mariel instructed, each word tersely uttered. "Now *move*."

The next second, there was a low *pop* and the gun flew out of Mariel's hand. With a stunned cry, Mariel pulled her hand away and sank to the floor. On her knees, she was rocking.

All of this took less than a second. Before Janelle could swing around to see what was going on behind her, Sawyer was in the room. Drawn service revolver in one hand, he grabbed her shoulder with the other.

"You okay?"

Was that tenderness? Concern? No, she was probably hallucinating. Numbly, Janelle nodded. "Yeah."

People began moving toward them down the hall. Mariel was still on her knees, still sobbing.

Releasing her shoulder, Sawyer backpedaled as he shook his head. "The minute I take my eyes off you…" He didn't bother finishing. Bending over, he picked up the weapon that Mariel had dropped. He was still talking to Janelle. "Don't you know that cowards are dangerous if you corner them?"

"I must have skipped that chapter," Janelle bit off. And then she sobered. That had been a miscalculation on her part. Her father would have her head—if he found out. "I thought I could handle her."

"You thought wrong," he snapped. "Our forefathers said it best— Guns are great equalizers."

"I didn't know she'd have one." Janelle pressed her lips together. She couldn't argue with him if he was right. And he had probably just saved her life. "Thanks."

Sawyer shrugged carelessly. As if his heart wasn't still doing double-time. As if everything hadn't suddenly frozen when he'd seen the short brunette pointing her gun at Janelle. He'd gotten up here as fast as he could, but when he'd seen the gun, he'd been afraid that it was already too late.

"Don't mention it."

"He made me do it," Mariel cried, clawing at the side of the desk for support as she tried to gain her feet. Standing, she swayed. "Wentworth. He said he'd kill my whole family if I didn't do what he wanted."

Sawyer regarded her coldly. One quick background check based on a hunch had laid it all out for him. "Did he also 'make' you take the money that put you through law school?"

Mariel's mouth dropped open as she stared at him, dumbfounded. He knew he'd hit a bull's-eye. The woman had probably thought no one would ever find out or make the connection. The arrogance of the criminal mind never ceased to amaze him.

"Hey, wait a minute," Janelle cried, grabbing his shoulder as people began to push their way into the room, firing questions that she tuned out. "How did you know that?"

Sawyer didn't get a chance to answer. Woods was

pushing his way through the crowd and into the office. He looked at the bleeding assistant, then at the gun in Sawyer's hand.

"What the hell is going on here?" Woods demanded, looking from Sawyer to Mariel to Janelle.

"We found your mole," she replied simply.

Mariel began to protest. Sawyer looked at her darkly. "You'll have your turn." The woman whimpered, but stopped talking.

Woods was completely stupefied. The information refused to process. "Mariel?"

Janelle nodded and produced Mariel's cell phone for Woods. "She's been making calls to Charlie Wentworth."

"Wentworth?" Woods echoed, confused. "But it's Wayne's son who's on trial—"

"We got caught in the middle of a power play, sir," Janelle explained. "Since Wayne looked like a shoo-in to succeed Salvatore Perelli when the old man retired or died, Wentworth threatened Wayne, telling him to back off and to toe the line. When Wayne told him where to go, Wentworth played hardball, striking Wayne in his only vulnerable place—his son. The drugs were planted to frame Tony."

The news caught the other members of the D.A.'s office by surprise. Voices rose as speculations were traded. Woods looked at Janelle skeptically. "And you know this how?"

Sawyer interrupted, taking the ball. "There were no fingerprints on the nickel bags we found in Junior's apartment. Except for one partial thumbprint." He turned to look at Mariel. "All government workers are fingerprinted. The print was yours."

It still didn't make any sense to her. "But why?" Janelle asked. "Why would you do something like that? What did he offer you?"

Sawyer didn't bother letting the woman make up excuses. He answered Janelle himself. "Wentworth's known Mariel since she was a baby," he told her. "She's his cousin's kid, from his old neighborhood. He took a special interest in her, sent her to law school and made her his eyes and ears in the D.A.'s office. Damn clever if you ask me." He could admire a man's technique and still loathe the man. "Lucky for us he got so impatient."

"You have no proof!" Mariel spat haughtily. Before their eyes, she transformed from a meek, agreeable assistant to a brazen young woman accustomed to getting her way. Accustomed to being privy to the machinations at the top. In his own fashion, Wentworth had doted on her. "This is all just desperate conjecture."

"If you want desperate," Janelle countered, "look into a mirror. And we have plenty of proof." She smiled and pointed to the cell phone. "In case you've forgotten how it works, we can subpoena phone records. Go back for years," she added, twisting the knife.

Mariel viciously cursed Janelle's parentage, then spit on her.

"Get her out of my sight," Woods ordered. "Someone call the jail and get a judge. I want the Wayne kid out before nightfall." He scrubbed his hand over his face, then ran it through his chestnut hair. "This is going to be embarrassing enough to deal with as it is." Woods shook his head, anticipating the future. "They'll probably slap the city with a lawsuit for wrongful arrest," he moaned.

Sawyer looked at Janelle. She thought she saw something akin to confidence in his eyes as he regarded her. "I think Cavanaugh can handle it so that doesn't happen."

Woods brightened ever so slightly. A light had appeared in the dark. "That's right, you have Wayne's ear, don't you?"

"More like he has—had—mine, sir," she corrected, thinking of the initial phone call. Woods's brow furrowed deeply. "But I'll see what I can do."

Woods nodded. "You do that, Janelle," the A.D.A. instructed, his voice both firm and weary at the same time. "You do that."

Two policemen approached, responding to a call placed by Woods's secretary. Mariel shrank back, but any escape was severely blocked. She looked at Woods, a frantic light in her eyes.

"You can't take me to jail," she cried, all her arrogance and bravado drained out of her.

Janelle smiled. "Wanna watch us?"

As the policeman snapped handcuffs on her, one of them beginning to recite the familiar words every suspect heard when taken into custody, Mariel jerked back. She almost flung herself in front of Sawyer. "I want immunity," she begged. "I want my family to be placed in protective custody."

"In exchange for?" Janelle asked before Woods could find his tongue.

Mariel took a deep breath. This time, Janelle believed that the nervous look on the woman's face was genuine. She was about to take a fateful step. Once she did, there would be no turning back. No return to the way things were before.

"A lot of inside information."

Sawyer regarded the woman for a long moment before his eyes shifted over toward Woods. "I think you might have found yourself a legitimate informant this time," he told the A.D.A.

Janelle couldn't remember the last time she'd seen Woods look so pleased.

Chapter 16

What remained of the afternoon moved at the clip of a commercial freight train making up for lost time. There was a tonnage of papers to file, a judge to coerce and a mountain to move. The wheels of justice turned slowly, but not this time.

Getting someone at the D.A.'s to cover for her in court, Janelle had spent the better part of the afternoon taking Mariel's statement. They wanted it fresh, before anyone could get to Mariel or she changed her mind. Janelle was far from finished when Woods had her pulled and replaced by one of the other assistants. She was stunned until she heard the reason why.

The moment the A.D.A received the green light on the paperwork, Woods chose Janelle to inform Anthony Wayne that he was free to go.

She knew Woods saw it as a reward for her part in finding the leak and preventing the D.A.'s office from suffering any further embarrassment. Operating under the assumption that everyone had his sense of values, Woods felt that she would be thrilled at being the bearer of good news as well as possibly snagging the spotlight.

But the spotlight had never meant very much to her. In addition, as she got into her car and drove the short distance to the local holding cell where Tony Wayne had been for the last two months, Janelle wasn't sure she could face the crime lieutenant's son now that she was aware of her connection to him.

Still, she couldn't exactly refuse without having a damn good reason.

Her conception had been an accident, she reminded herself. One that Marco Wayne would have easily brushed aside if that had been her mother's choice. He was only her father in the most technical sense. She might share DNA with him and his offspring, but that didn't make Tony her brother. Time, love and life did that.

She had three brothers. She wasn't looking for more. Now if only her stomach could understand that.

Arriving at the police department, a building she had walked into so many times she couldn't possibly begin to count, she felt nervous for the first time in her life. She doubted that Marco had told Tony about his affair with her mother. That put her one up on the younger Wayne.

As it should be.

Taking in several deep breaths, she put her hand out in front of her. It was steady.

Okay, here we go.

She hurried into the building and hoped she wouldn't run into anyone she knew.

But she did.

Sawyer, who had left her shortly after coming to her rescue, seemed to materialize out of nowhere and fell into step with her as she went to the room reserved for defense attorneys and their clients.

"What are you doing here?" she asked. Damn, just what she needed, to have her pulse rate go up another few notches. She'd be lucky if she made it through today intact.

"In case you hadn't noticed," he said, holding the door open for her, "this is the police department building."

She made a right turn down the corridor that led to the very back of the building and the holding cells. "I *know* what it is," she retorted, "but what are you doing *here?*" She waved her hand around at the specific area.

The soft hint of a smile shot right through her. "Didn't think I'd let you go in here alone, did you?"

Did he know? she wondered. Did he suspect how nervous she was about this meeting? How had he gotten into her head so easily?

"He's not dangerous," she pointed out.

"Didn't say he was," Sawyer said, taking hold of her arm.

Reflexes and the independent streak that she had nurtured ever since she was old enough to dress herself would have had her pulling her arm away. But reflexes were trumped by inherent instincts. Janelle left her arm where it was, allowing Sawyer to guide her into the small conference room.

Along with his lawyer, Anthony Wayne was brought in less than two minutes later. Janelle sat up even straighter in her chair. The younger man looked nothing like his father. Thin-boned and slight, she could only assume that the man she had seen only once before, at his arraignment, took after his mother.

As she took after hers, she thought.

Edward Parnell, who took the chair beside Tony, was as sharp as they came. He was also, like the custom-made suits he wore, the best that money could buy.

"You have news for us?" Parnell directed his inquiry to Janelle, his body language indicating that he was oblivious to the police detective with her.

Rather than address the attorney, Janelle looked at her half brother, wondering if anyone was ever going to tell him of their connection. She sincerely hoped not. Life was complicated enough as it was without her having to deal with that.

She folded her hands before her. *He's a kid and he's scared.* Suddenly, she was glad she was the one bringing him this news. "New evidence has recently come to the attention of the district attorney's office. You were framed, Mr. Wayne, and now you're free to go."

He stared at her, as if afraid to believe what he was hearing. His voice was almost reedy and nearly broke as he asked, "Just like that?"

She nodded. "Assistant D.A. Woods rushed through the paperwork personally. Judge Winterset signed off on it." She smiled at Tony, feeling compassionate stirrings despite everything she'd told herself just prior to walking into the room. "Everything's in order. As of three o'clock this afternoon, all charges against you were dropped." She added the necessary coda. "You have the sincerest apologies of the city of Aurora."

"Not good enough," Parnell said.

She'd expected nothing less from the attorney. Neither did Woods. She knew the man was preparing for battle.

"You'll have to take that up with the D.A.'s office," she told him as she rose from the table. She was aware of Sawyer rising as well. The police detective had surprised her with his silence. Janelle hooked her purse straps on her shoulder and pushed her chair in. "I'm just the messenger."

Very obviously shaky, Tony Wayne rose to his feet as well. "Miss—"

"Cavanaugh," she told him, the coolness leaving her voice. "Janelle Cavanaugh."

"Miss Cavanaugh," Tony repeated, then hesitated before he asked, "do I know you?"

She wondered about that old saying, *Blood will out,* and if it actually meant anything. "We met at your arraignment."

But Tony shook his head. "Besides that."

Yes, I'm your sister. Your half sister, but there's no way for you to know that. So she smiled and shook her head as well. "No."

He looked reluctant to accept that as his final answer. "Funny, I had this feeling…"

Her smile was compassionate as it widened. Janelle crossed back for a moment and made physical contact, squeezing his hand. "That's probably just the heady smell of freedom getting to you. Don't do anything to lose it," she counseled. With that, she turned away and headed toward the outer door.

"We'll be in touch," Parnell called after her as she and Sawyer left the room.

"I'm sure you will be, Mr. Parnell," she said under her breath.

It wasn't until she and Sawyer were outside the building and Janelle had taken in a deep breath that she finally looked at the man who had been at her side the whole time, as silent as a grave. Despite that, she had to admit that she had been glad that she hadn't been alone in that room.

"Well, you certainly didn't say a word the whole time." He was never very chatty, but he'd always said *something*.

"No need to. You were doing just fine on your own." A corner of his mouth lifted a fraction. "I was just the shadow on the wall."

Janelle came to a stop by her car and turned around. "You would *never* be just a shadow on the wall," she contradicted. "You're much too dynamic for that."

Amusement highlighted his features, softening them. "Is that a compliment?"

She hadn't intended to make a big deal out of it, just an observation. And, okay, a compliment she grudgingly admitted. "What, it's been so long since you heard one you don't know a compliment when you get one?" She took a breath, then said, "Yes, that was a compliment."

The amusement didn't dissipate as he continued to regard her closer than she felt comfortable. He seemed to be in her space without actually physically occupying it. "I just didn't think you were wired that way."

"What way?"

He leaned a hip against her car. "To give a man his due."

She did too give a man his due. She just didn't believe in going overboard. The male ego, in her opinion, tended to overinflate at times. "There are nine men in my family. I choose my moments." She glanced at her watch. "Technically, I'm off the clock."

He nodded. It was after five. "I was never on. Vacation," he reminded her.

Suddenly, with the burden of the Wayne problem behind her, she needed to know things. "So, what now?"

"Dinner?" Sawyer suggested. His voice was casual. The complete antithesis of how he felt inside. "There's this little steak house at the edge of town that serves the best steaks at a decent price—"

She shook her head. "No, I mean 'what now?'" Where did that leave them? The personal *them* that had emerged out of the professional *them*. "I don't need anyone watching my back anymore. The Wayne case is over."

He crossed his arms before him and began to speak, then stopped, waiting for an approaching policeman to pass them before continuing. "Are we having 'the talk,' Cavanaugh?"

She stiffened immediately, regretting what she'd just said. "The talk?"

His expression gave nothing away and added to her

sense of discomfort. She'd crawled out on a limb and found herself alone out there.

"Yeah," he said, "the one where the woman wants to know where the relationship is going."

More than anything else, Janelle hated stereotyping. Hated being seen in such narrow parameters. "Never mind," she told him. All she wanted to do now was just go home. Alone. "I never said anything. The steak house sounds pretty good, but—"

"Because if we are—having the talk," he clarified when she glared at him, "then I'd have to say that it's going to go wherever you want it to go."

That stopped her in her tracks mentally if not physically. She hadn't expected him to say that and was afraid that she was still misunderstanding him.

"What?"

"You been listening to loud music and blowing out your eardrums?" His sober expression hid the uncertainty he was experiencing. "I said—"

"I heard what you said," she interrupted, irritated. What did he want from her? Was he setting her up? Getting her to make an admission so that he could have the last laugh at her expense? Damn it, ever since she'd found out about her roots, she'd lost her confidence in her ability to make the right call. To *be* right. "I just don't understand what you mean by it."

He studied her for a moment before asking, "What part confused you?"

Okay, he wanted to be a smart-ass, she'd treat him like one. "The part where you said the relationship was going to go wherever I wanted it to go. First of all, I wasn't aware that we even *had* a relationship—"

"You always cure your hiccups by making love with whoever you're with?"

She ignored the interruption and kept going. "And second, you're not going to place the burden of this on me and then just pretend to be the innocent bystander here."

He raised an eyebrow. "Burden?"

"Okay," she bit off grudgingly, "poor choice of word. You like *responsibility* better?"

The wind ruffled the stray strands that had worked their way loose from the confining pins she'd fastened in her hair. He was tempted to pull them out and then move his fingers through her hair.

"I'd like it better if you took that chip off your shoulder," he told her.

Janelle closed her mouth, her retort dying with the action. He was right. She was acting as if she had a chip on her shoulder. But that was the fear talking. The fear that she was in the presence of something rare and that she would somehow ruin it, scare it away, before she ever had a chance to cultivate it.

"Okay," she agreed quietly, conceding his point.

"And," he continued in the same tone, "took the clothes off your body."

A giddiness worked its way to the surface as her mood instantly lightened. Janelle almost laughed out loud. "Here?"

Very slowly, he glided his fingertips along her face, pushing one small strand of hair out of her eyes. "Preferably your place or my place, but here if you really feel you can't wait to jump my bones."

The breath she drew felt short. But she managed to look nonchalant. Just barely. "I think I can contain myself."

His eyes held hers. "You're sure?"

She didn't like him having the upper hand. Because he did. "I'm sure."

"Because," Sawyer continued as if she hadn't answered him, "I'm finding I'm having trouble containing myself." He looked at her pointedly, admitting things he knew he should have kept to himself. "That's never happened before."

Sawyer wasn't the type to string a woman along, or feed her lines, Janelle thought. Instinctively, she knew that about him. The man didn't like lies. Which meant he was telling her the truth. She could feel her pulse accelerating again.

"No?"

He was leaving himself open, Sawyer thought. Vulnerable. He was asking for trouble. And pain. And yet, he couldn't just turn away. It was too late for that. Coming back and finding Mariel pointing a gun at Janelle had showed him that.

"No."

Janelle inclined her head. "I guess I'm honored then."

"You certainly are something," he said almost under his breath. Just then, as if to cool a mood that was swiftly heating up, her cell phone rang. Mentally, Janelle cursed it, and Sawyer dropped his hand. "Maybe you'd better get that," he suggested.

Suppressing her impatience, Janelle pulled the small cell phone out of her purse. It took everything she had not to snap out her name. "Cavanaugh."

"Thank you."

There was no preamble. There didn't have to be. She immediately knew who the deep voice belonged to, even though she'd never given her number to the man on the other end of her phone.

It astounded her that he could have found out so quickly what was going on. But then, people in his line of work had to be quick. Their lives often depended on it.

Janelle chose her words carefully. "You kept out of my mother's life. Consider us even."

"You want it that way?" Wayne asked.

The unspoken part of her statement asked for him to stay out of her life as well. "I think it would be best."

There was a long pause on the other end. For a moment, Janelle thought Wayne would give her an argument, try to convince her that they should keep in touch now that there was no longer a secret between them.

"Yeah, me, too," Wayne finally said. "Take care of yourself, kid. And tell Brian he did a good job."

"I'll pass that along," she assured him. The next second, the dial tone hummed softly in her ear. With a shake of her head, she slipped the phone back into her purse.

Sawyer peered at her face. "Wayne?" he guessed.

"Boy, nothing gets past you," she said with a short laugh, but for once she hadn't meant the remark sarcastically. "Wayne," she confirmed, looking at Sawyer. The nerves were back in full regalia. She liked it better when she just thought of the man as an annoying inconvenience rather than someone whose presence in her world had come to mean so much. It was easier the other way. "So, where were we?"

He traced a tendril along her temple. "You were just about to get naked."

It took effort to control the shiver that danced up and down her spine at the image of the two of them that suggestion evoked. She did her best to sound flippant. "No, I wasn't."

"Not even if I bribe you with dinner?" he asked.

"You might stand a better chance that way," Janelle allowed. And then the humor temporarily left her eyes. "Sawyer—"

Her tone of voice had him feeling leery. He tried, for once, not to expect the worst. "Yeah?"

She faced him squarely, even though the subject made her uncomfortable. "I don't do this kind of thing normally."

"Eat dinner?" he asked innocently.

"You know what I mean," she retorted impatiently. Then her voice lowered. "Sleep around casually."

Humor glinted in his eyes. "I wasn't aware that naked was considered formal."

Embarrassed, angry, she was sorry she'd said anything. "If this is going to be a joke—" Janelle tried to yank open the driver's side door only to have him push it shut again.

"It's because there's this river rushing over me and I'm trying to tread water here as fast as I can." He put his hands on her shoulders, forcing her to look at him. "I was in love once, with Allison, and when she died, it was like having all my guts ripped out. It just about killed me. I don't want to be in love again."

"No one's telling you to be in love," she retorted defensively.

He shook his head. "You don't get it, do you? Nobody can tell you to be in love, you either are, or you're not."

"Okay." Janelle drew the word out slowly as she tried to absorb what he was attempting to get across.

His hands moved from her shoulders to head, cupping her face. "And I am."

"With me?" she whispered.

Nervous impatience shot through him. "No, with A.D.A. Woods. Of course with you. Now, I don't know where this is going to take us—"

"Sawyer," Janelle tried to cut in, but Sawyer just continued talking.

"—and I'll probably screw up—"

"Sawyer—"

"—but, then, maybe—"

"*Sawyer.*"

He stopped abruptly. Why wasn't she letting him finish? "What?"

She slipped her arms around his neck, bringing her body tantalizingly close to his. "I love you, too. Now shut up and take me to your place so that I can get naked without drawing a crowd."

He grinned. "A crowd, huh? Think pretty highly of yourself, don't you?"

Janelle looked up at him, her eyes serious. "Don't you?"

"Yeah," he replied, pulling her even more closely to him, "I do." He kissed her. Slowly. Tenderly. Then raised his head and repeated the last two words he'd said. "I do."

There was mischief in her eyes. Mischief and such a wave of excitement it almost overwhelmed her. "Careful where you say those words," she advised.

"Just practicing."

Janelle stared, dumbfounded. But before she could ask him if he meant what she thought he meant, Sawyer was kissing her again. And stealing the very breath away from her.

* * * * *

Don't miss Marie Ferrarella's next romance,
Mother in Training,
available October 2007
from Mills & Boon Special Edition.

Once a Thief

by

Michele Hauf

French countryside—Location: undisclosed
5:55 a.m.

Sooty, the sunless morning sky. Rain beat upon a dented metal awning scrolled over the study windows. A yard light mounted on a rusted flagpole sketched a haze of blurry gold across the grassless, muddy courtyard.

The limestone facade of the Lazar compound offered a sheer three-story rise facing east. The windows were matte gray, no lights behind them. Raindrops pattered the tin air vents spotting the red-tile roof.

Off-road tires had impressed fresh parallel trails in the mud; the household crew—but a cook and groundsman—had left for the nearest village half an hour earlier to collect supplies for the week.

The day always began before dawn. Rachel could not remember a time when it had not. Hop from bed, meditate with tai chi, down a protein breakfast and then to run laps, or—if raining like today—go to the gym to lift weights. Routine kept her body hard, her mind sound and her vision focused. Vision, having nothing to do with eyesight and everything to do with the purpose of her life—to follow orders and to be nothing less than the best. A machine. Christian Lazar's pretty machine.

Today, a sporting match of blades had been offered—in the usual you-know-better-than-to-refuse tone. Refusal hadn't entered her mind. Rachel enjoyed the rain. The challenge and exhilaration of the weather had spurred on both opponents.

Now Rachel crouched in the center of the courtyard. Cold November rain beat down from the lightening morning sky. Her long black hair, secured tightly in a ponytail with a wrap of thin leather strips, sat heavily upon her right shoulder. Her Doc Martens were slick with mud, as well as her black pants. The ultrathin jacket she wore as protection against a swift and cocky blade—fashioned from gabardine and Kevlar—repelled the rain in speedy rivulets.

Propping her elbows on her knees and bowing her head, Rachel closed her eyes. A shiver encompassed her body. She was not chilled, but unsettled.

In the shadows of the timber soffit Christian sat—no, he didn't sit—he had collapsed.

Could he be dead?

Water dribbled off Rachel's nose and in the curve of her upper lip. Splaying one hand over her knee, her fingertips shot out pearls of rain. Concern niggled, beating out a reluctant empathy. So difficult to show compassion, yet the compulsion was there.

Snippets of last night's conversation with Christian eddied inside her skull. He'd quietly entered her small, spare bedroom. Rachel hadn't realized he'd settled next to her on the ironwood bench until he'd remarked on the absence of koi in the pond outside her floor-to-ceiling window. Garland, the groundsman, had been cleaning the pond and had removed the three giant fish for the winter.

Levity had softened Christian's tone. A rare occurrence. *Beware.*

After moments of silent reflection, the two of them sitting facing the window, staring at the still pond, he'd cleared his throat. Then, with a slow start, but gaining confidence, he'd actually asked what Rachel had wanted to be when she was a child.

The question had stunned her. But she had learned long ago to simply answer, never argue a query, no matter how conversational it sounded.

"I don't know," Rachel had answered. Had she ever been a child? So much he had taken from her. *You allowed it to be taken.* "Doesn't matter anymore. I am…what I have become."

Christian leaned forward and pressed a palm to the cool glass—the window spanned one complete wall of her room and viewed the miniparadise outside. His fingers were long, elegant, but powerful. Capable of cutting off breath, of snapping a collarbone. He remained beside her, too far to touch, too close to disregard. Breaths moved in soft rhythm from his chest. Always, his presence was impeccable, precise, tainted only by the warm spice from the soap he used. Rachel could feel him on her skin, taste him in her throat. Predatory, his sensuality, and so dangerous.

"What of you?" a destructive curiosity had made her wonder. The little girl lost inside her cringed. "What made you the man you are today?"

He'd answered after a few beats. "The same thing that made you what you are."

She had suspected as much. Trained. *Don't falter. Concen-*

trate. You cannot achieve success without sweat, struggle and yes, blood. This is what you are meant to be. Brutal mastery of a naive and frightened teenager. *No one cared for you. I do. Only I love you, Rachel Blu.*

A cruel love, that.

And then she had dared ask, "How did you…get away from him?"

She had *heard* Christian's grin—a little exhale of air from his nose, and then that slight lift of his mouth on the left side. Evil, that grin.

"I killed him."

Now Rachel tucked her head down and twisted to search the rain-distorted shadows dancing against the east wall of the compound. Was Christian dead? *I killed him.* No, she would not think it. She was no murderer. Life was too precious. The machine that she had become had not been programmed to kill.

She and Christian had been fencing. Not a friendly spar, but instead a no-holds-barred teaching experience that ever impressed her of Christian's skills. *Still more powerful than you.*

Fencing wasn't a practical skill—not in this age of high-caliber weapons and extreme martial arts—but it did teach balance and build stamina, and it forced you to prethink your moves, to learn to anticipate the opponent's next move, or two. The slightest miscalculation could result in injury; as the scar on Rachel's jaw attested.

When the downpour began, Christian had reveled in the challenge. As had Rachel. She liked to test her body's limits. The mud and cold did not disappoint. Mud suctioned every footstep, and intermittent spots of wet grass tested her balance. They'd been fencing for half an hour; had ignored the crew's leave for market.

Then it had happened—jaw tight, Christian had let out a yelp and clutched his forehead.

Rachel's initial thought was to run to him—brief, that moment of compassion—but conditioning had taught her to staunchly stand back. Hide emotion. Hold your war stance. Never let the opponent see there may be weakness lurking within.

I am not weak. I am a survivor.

In the next instant, Christian began to fall, the rapier still gripped in his outstretched hand, ready to deflect the riposte Rachel hadn't finished. His shoulder hit the ground first. Mud splattered his eyelids. A spasm rocked him to his back where he now lay half in, half out of shadow. His legs were visible in the glow beaming down from the rusted metal yard light.

Tentatively, Rachel had stepped across the courtyard and bent over him, extending a hand to touch—

—retract.

Wide, empty blue eyes. Unblinking. Dark lashes deflected the raindrops. Did he see her? What had happened? She hadn't completed the riposte. Her blade had gone nowhere near his face, yet he'd clutched his head.

Could it be? The migraines. At rare times Christian would closet himself away in his room. No entrance. Punishment waited should she make noise.

The cook had reluctantly revealed Christian's debilitating secret years earlier after Rachel had threatened her with a hot frying pan. *He doesn't want you to know about them. One of these days one of those nasty head pains will kill him.* Rachel would not have hurt the woman, but she knew the value of a threat.

Still squatting, Rachel lifted her head, keeping her back to the fallen man. Sweet, the rain's fragrance, like a wide-open field. Lightly, it fell in her heart.

After all this time, had the moment finally been granted? *This is it! You've been planning for this day. Ever since...* "I know you love me," Christian had said one night many

months earlier. (Or had it been years? So difficult to track tim
here in Christian's world away from society.) The last birth
day she had celebrated was her sweet sixteen. Not so swee
she recalled. Calculating in his devotion, Christian's ice-blu
eyes held a flame frozen in their centers. "As well, I know
your hate for me is equal to the love. That's the way it shoul
be. Black and white. No gray. Never think you can walk awa
from me, Rachel Blu." Whenever he used her middle nam
it cemented the fact he knew so much more about her tha
she could begin to know about him. Rachel Blu, spoken i
his claiming whisper, had become a vile oath over the years
"I made you, Rachel Blu. I *am* you."

Always he held the upper hand. She had believed in him
She loved him. Yes, he had made her. Christian had taken he
from an ugly life and placed her into his own. A machine, h
often admiringly said of her. "My pretty machine."

But for all he had given Rachel, the one thing he'd denie
her—intimacy—cleaved at her soul.

Just one kiss, please?

Always denied. Sex was required—a tool used to gain ad
vantage over a mark—but to press together their mouths vi
olated the invisible boundaries Christian kept secured abou
him.

And so Rachel had begun to make plans. To invest in hope

Everything was ready. She needn't much. A change o
clothing, some cash and her passports. The few other neces
sities she had inventoried were locked in Christian's safe—
an easy crack.

Decisive, Rachel stood and eased back her shoulders t
stretch the muscles chilled by the rain. Realizing she sti
held the rapier, she thrust it forward. It landed in a growing
puddle with a tinny splash.

"Touché?" she whispered, so unsure of this gift of victory

How much time before the cook and Garland—more a pe

riphery guard than the gardener, for he did pack heat—returned? Another hour, tops. They'd taken the off-road, but the Clio remained in the car shed.

Escape? She needed but ten minutes.

Twisting to face the fallen man—her teacher, her mentor, her lover, her tormentor—Rachel shrugged off the Kevlar jacket and dangled it in her left hand. Rain soaked through her thin cotton muscle shirt. Two paces placed her over the prone body of a man she truly did hate as much as she loved. Love confused. Hate, well, that was a prime bit of high, wasn't it?

Lifting a boot to toe Christian's leg, she paused. A touch might wake him from a mere faint. Too risky.

She ran her palm up her left arm and shivered. Short breaths misted before her. Strange, she'd just noticed how cold the rain actually was. Beneath her palm she felt the raised lines in the bulge of her bicep—two inserts half an inch long and thin as a toothpick—just below her skin. Tracking devices implanted when she had first arrived at the ranch.

I'll always know where you are, Rachel Blu.

Slipping a hand over her sodden clothing, she glided her fingers into the back pocket of her pants. The small leaf-shaped push dagger fitted into her palm and with a flick, she exposed the blade.

Now, to forever remove Christian Lazar from her life.

FREE

4 BOOKS AND A SURPRISE GIFT!

We would like to take this opportunity to thank you for reading this Mills & Boon® book by offering you the chance to take FOUR more specially selected titles from the Intrigue™ series absolutely FREE! We're also making this offer to introduce you to the benefits of the Mills & Boon® Reader Service™—

- ★ **FREE home delivery**
- ★ **FREE gifts and competitions**
- ★ **FREE monthly Newsletter**
- ★ **Books available before they're in the shops**
- ★ **Exclusive Reader Service offers**

Accepting these FREE books and gift places you under no obligation to buy; you may cancel at any time, even after receiving your free shipment. Simply complete your details below and return the entire page to the address below. You don't even need a stamp!

YES! Please send me 4 free Intrigue books and a surprise gift. I understand that unless you hear from me, I will receive 6 superb new titles every month for just £3.10 each, postage and packing free. I am under no obligation to purchase any books and may cancel my subscription at any time. The free books and gift will be mine to keep in any case.

I7ZEE

Ms/Mrs/Miss/Mr......................................Initials ....

BLOCK CAPITALS PLEASE

Surname ....

Address ....

....

....Postcode ....

Send this whole page to:
The Reader Service, FREEPOST CN81, Croydon, CR9 3WZ